Lemonade
and Lies

A Peridale Cafe
MYSTERY

AGATHA FROST

A Peridale Cafe MYSTERY

Book Two

CHAPTER 1

J ulia awoke to the sound of banging again. She stared at her bedroom ceiling, darkness suffocating her vision. She tossed and turned, clutching at her eyes, forgetting she was wearing an eye mask. The first hints of the oncoming sunrise were slipping through the darkness. It was earlier in the morning than she would like to acknowledge.

Yanking off her eye mask, she looked at the dark beams in her small cottage's low ceiling. Another low thud echoed through the darkness to remind her why she had awoken.

Julia tossed back her satin duvet and slid her feet into the warm sheepskin slippers her gran had given to her for Christmas. She stood up, her knees creaking more with each day. A quick glance in the mirror at her pale pink nightie and her wild curly hair reminded her that she was only thirty-seven. She wouldn't have to start worrying about her knees giving way for another couple of years, or so she hoped. She thought of her octogenarian gran, who was still darting around the village like a woman in her twenties.

She hurried along the hallway, a chill brushing against her exposed legs. Her grey Maine Coon, Mowgli, was softly purring in a fluffy ball on the doormat, unaware of the night-time disturbance.

Julia stopped outside of her guest bedroom, which was currently being occupied by her new sixteen-year-old lodger, Jessika, who went by the name Jessie. Julia had never expected to take a young girl into her home, but she also hadn't expected to find that same girl breaking into her café and stealing cakes on a regular basis. Julia could have taken the homeless girl to the police, but she decided to do the kinder thing. She gave the girl a home, and a job helping out in Julia's café.

Hovering her knuckles over the wood, she almost knocked, but she decided against waking Jessie. She knew how dangerous that could be for a sleepwalker.

Julia pried open Jessie's bedroom door as silently as she could, which wasn't easy in the centuries old cottage. She felt the entire timber frame scream out, a piercing creak cracking like a whip through the silence. In the corner of her eye, Mowgli looked up from his slumber, before tucking his nose back under his paw.

Jessie had been living with Julia for nearly a month but the sleepwalking was new. This was the fourth time it had woken Julia. She had felt useless to help her young lodger at first, but after a quick internet search, she was more equipped to deal with the situation.

She made out the shadow of Jessie through the dark as she delicately and rhythmically pounded her head against her wardrobe door. Her long, dark hair hung over her face, contrasting against her stark white nightie, making her look like she had crawled out of the screen of a horror film. Julia wasn't scared; she was just an ordinary girl after all.

Julia did the only thing she could do. She placed

her hand between Jessie's forehead and the wood, softening the blow. As though she could consciously sense the change, the movement stopped, but she didn't wake. Without saying a word, Julia guided Jessie back to her bed, which she climbed back into with ease. It hadn't been as simple the night before.

After tucking Jessie back in, Julia gazed down at the girl, wondering how she had survived living on the streets for so long. Jessie hadn't talked much about it, so Julia hadn't asked, but it didn't mean she wasn't curious.

Julia turned and spotted a book on Jessie's nightstand. The cover and title made her smile. She picked up '*Baking For Beginners*' and flicked to the front page. It seemed that Jessie had borrowed it from Peridale's tiny library without Julia's knowledge. In the weeks Jessie had been working in the café, she had been clearing tables, washing up, and assisting in Julia's baking. Julia could sense Jessie was itching to get her hands properly stuck into baking her own creations.

When she seemed at peace in bed, Julia placed the cookbook exactly where she had found it. She backed out of the room, cautiously closing the creaking door. She walked past her own bedroom and straight into the kitchen. She dropped one of her favourite peppermint and liquorice teabags into a cup and filled the kettle.

She flicked on her under-counter lights and pulled up a stool. The cat clock with the flickering eyes and swishing tail told her it was a little after six. Letting out a slow yawn, she knew she would pay for her early start later in the café. Saturdays were always the busiest days but at least she had Jessie's help now.

Julia cast her eyes to the white envelope sitting on the corner of her counter. The divorce papers enclosed within had been read over and signed, and the envelope resealed ready for posting to her solicitor. She wanted to post them, but just like a bad cold, she was finding it difficult to get rid of them.

The moment they were with her solicitor again, she would be divorced. Considering she didn't much like her soon-to-be ex-husband, she should have been happy about finally cutting ties from him, but happiness was an emotion that evaded anything surrounding the break up. More than anything, she felt she had failed, not just her marriage, but herself. She had changed so much and abandoned her village to join her husband, Jerrad, in London. Twelve years later, she found her bags on the doorstep along with a note telling her he had changed the locks because he was in love with his secretary, who was ten years Julia's junior and twenty pounds lighter around the middle.

Two years later, Julia now owned her small cottage on the outskirts of Peridale, the village she had grown up in. She had opened her own café in the heart of the community, and now she had a lodger, as well as her cat. She felt she was truly content with her life, which didn't explain to her why she was clinging onto the envelope.

Tossing back the last of her tea, she cursed herself under her breath. She promised herself today would be the day she dropped them in at the post office.

No more excuses.

Jessie woke with her alarm clock at eight. The sun was high in the clear sky and Julia was already washed and dressed for work. She had also already made good progress with her usual morning baking to fill the display cases in her café.

"This was on the doormat," Jessie grumbled as she scratched her hair, flinging a lavender envelope on top of the divorce papers. "I had the craziest dream last night."

"Oh?" Julia asked, avoiding Jessie's still half-closed eyes. "What about?"

"It's already gone," Jessie said with a shrug. "What are you baking?"

"I'm trying to perfect Sally and Richard's wedding cake recipe," Julia said, pushing a finished cupcake in front of Jessie. "I just can't seem to get the balance right."

Jessie took a big bite out of the cupcake. Julia didn't have to wait long for the verdict. Jessie immediately spat the mixture back into the cake casing and pulled a face that reminded Julia of the time Mowgli licked chilli powder off the counter.

"Oh, God. What's in that?"

"Cinnamon, orange and rose," Julia said with a heavy sigh, looking at the dozen cupcakes she had just baked, hoping to be able to sell them in the café. "I might just have to tell Sally it can't be done. Was there too much rose?"

"There was too much everything," Jessie said, shaking her head, looking down at the cupcake with disgust. "Who wants a cinnamon, orange and rose wedding cake, anyway?"

Julia had to wonder. She was often people's first port of call when they wanted a wedding cake but didn't want to pay the out of town bakery prices.

Julia prided herself on her baking, humbly accepting that she was the best baker in the village, but even she sometimes got it wrong. She had quickly learned she could count on Jessie to tell the truth. She was a girl who did not mince her words.

"Can I have one of your fancy teabag things?" Jessie asked as she wandered over to the kettle. "And some painkillers? My head is banging."

Julia fished two painkillers out of her designation junk drawer in her kitchen, and slid them across the counter to Jessie. She thought about telling her about the sleepwalking, but she didn't want to alarm her. Julia was hoping it would stop before it got too serious, but from her research, it could be a recurring problem that usually intensified when somebody was under extreme pressure or stress. Julia thought giving Jessie a home and a job had taken that stress off her young shoulders. Had she given her too much responsibility too soon?

Julia sat at the counter and pulled a corner off one of the cupcakes. As usual, Jessie had been right about the overpowering flavour. It wasn't often her baking found its way straight into the bin, but these were nowhere near the high standard the villagers of Peridale expected from her café.

Jessie put a cup of peppermint and liquorice tea

in front of Julia, and pulled up the chair next to her. Julia turned her attention to the lavender coloured envelope, suddenly realising it was far too early for the postman to have made his way up to her cottage.

"You found this on the doormat?" Julia asked as she picked up the envelope.

"That's what I said."

Julia turned it over in her hands. It had no stamp, and it was simply addressed to '*Julia*' in such ornate and delicate lettering it resembled art.

"Who hand delivers letters this early in the morning?" Julia wondered aloud.

"A nutter. I'm going for a shower. I smell like Mowgli after he's been rolling in the garden."

Leaving her tea unfinished, Jessie shuffled to the bathroom, and it wasn't long before rushing water and the sound of Jessie's singing floated through the cottage. Julia smiled to herself. She had come to enjoy Jessie's company more than she had expected.

After taking a sip of her hot tea, Julia tore open the tight seal of the envelope, the overpowering scent of lavender filling her nostrils. She winced. Her mother had hated the smell of lavender and Julia had inherited that quirk. As she pulled the letter out of the envelope, Mowgli jumped up onto the counter. He sniffed the unfinished cupcake, then the letter;

he turned his nose up at both.

"Alright, I get it!" she said, tickling under Mowgli's chin. "It's awful!'

The heavily scented letter appeared to be an invitation, handwritten in the same ornate lettering as her name on the envelope. She scanned the invitation, her eyes honing in on the signature at the bottom. Her stomach knotted when she saw '*Katie Wellington-South*'.

Starting back at the top where her own name was, she read through the detailed invitation:

Dear Julia,

It gives me great pleasure to invite you to Peridale Manor for a very special garden party, where I, Katie Wellington-South, and my dear husband, Brian South, will be making an exciting announcement.

Please arrive at Peridale Manor at noon on Sunday March 11th. You are welcome to bring one guest.

We look forward to your attendance, and we cannot wait to share our very special news with you.

With hugs and kisses,
Katie Wellington-South

Lemonade and Lies

Julia didn't know how many times she read over the invitation, picking over every word, trying to decode what secrets were going to be revealed at the '*very special garden party*'. She didn't like where her imagination was taking her.

"Katie Wellington-South?" Jessie mumbled as she read the invitation over Julia's shoulder, breaking her from her thoughts. "Who's that?"

"My father's wife," Julia said, pushing the scented paper back into its envelope. "She's inviting us to a garden party tomorrow."

"Don't you mean your step-mother?" Jessie asked as she rubbed a towel through her dark hair. "I've been with enough families to know your dad's missus is your step-mum."

"Katie Wellington is *not* my step-mother," Julia said quickly. "Come on, get dressed. We're going to be late to open the café."

Jessie rolled her eyes and headed off to her bedroom, leaving Julia to read over the note again. When her sister and gran both called one after the other asking if she too had received an invitation, she was only surprised it had taken them so long to call.

"Are you going?" Sue had asked.

"Are you going?" her gran had asked.

Julia had given them both the same response.

"I don't know."

And she didn't. As they drove towards the centre of Peridale village with the morning's bakes carefully fastened in on the backseat, Julia drummed her fingers on the steering wheel, wondering what kind of announcement could be so important that it needed a garden party to make it. In the depths of her mind, she heard the sound of a baby crying, and every hair on her body stood on end.

It wasn't until she was pulling into her parking space between her café and the post office that she realised she had, once again, forgotten to pick up the divorce papers off the kitchen counter.

CHAPTER 2

J ulia was surprised to find herself at Peridale
Manor the next morning. Looking up at the
sandstone bricks of the old enormous manor
house, she felt comfort in knowing most of the
village had also received hand delivered lavender
invitations. One of the many perks of owning a café
was that Julia didn't have to seek out gossip, it
usually found her.

"You've never spoken about your dad before," Jessie said carefully, appearing to sense Julia's tension. "Are you close?"

"Not anymore," Julia said, her fingers tightening around the Victoria sponge cake she had baked that morning. "Should we ring the doorbell? I'm surprised more people aren't here yet."

Julia checked her silver wristwatch, wondering why she had thought it was a good idea to get there an hour early. She had hoped to ease herself into the day, but she hadn't expected to be the only one to show up so soon.

"Maybe we should wait in the car for more people to show?" Jessie suggested, hooking her thumb back to Julia's vintage aqua blue Ford Anglia, which was sitting quietly on the gravel driveway.

"That might look a little odd."

"And standing on the doorstep doesn't? What's so bad about your dad and his missus anyway?"

Before Julia could answer, Jessie jabbed a finger on the ivory doorbell. It tinkled throughout the house, bouncing off the various wooden and marble surfaces that Julia knew lay beyond the front door. Jessie unapologetically winked at Julia, and stuffed her hands into the pockets of her scruffy jeans. She had refused Julia's offer of driving to the late-night mall out of town to buy a dress for the occasion.

The door opened and Julia was relieved not to see Katie or her father. Instead, the flushed and frowning face of someone she assumed was the housekeeper greeted them.

"Yes?" the short, dumpy woman snapped, her fierce eyes darting from Julia to Jessie, then to the cake tin. "The garden party doesn't start for another an hour. You'll have to come back later. We're not ready."

Julia knew most faces in the village, but she didn't recognise this one. The woman's lined skin and pulled back wiry hair made it obvious she should have taken her retirement long ago. Charcoal black lined her bulging eyes, making them look like they could pop out and roll down the driveway at any moment.

"She's family," Jessie said, offense loud in her voice. "The Lord of the Manor's daughter. Isn't that right, Julia?"

"Mr. Wellington?" the woman snapped, looking Julia up and down, her wide eyes somehow continuing to widen. "Mr. Wellington only has one daughter, and *this* is certainly not her."

Julia was glad there was nothing wrong with the elderly woman's eyesight. She would hate to be mistaken for Katie Wellington.

"What Jessie was *trying* to say, is that I'm Brian's daughter," Julia said, applying her best smile and offering forth the Victoria sponge cake. "Mr. South?"

"I know whom you're talking about," the woman snapped, shaking her hand, then stepping to the side. "You had better come in. Funny, I never knew he had a daughter."

"He's got two," Jessie said, stepping over the threshold without wiping her feet on the doormat. "Nice gaff you've got here."

"The correct thing to say would be '*he has two daughters*', not '*got*'. And it is a '*manor*', not a '*gaff*', whatever that means," the woman said bitterly, hurrying Julia into the house so she could close the door. "You really should teach your daughter proper English."

"She's not my mum," Jessie said casually as she spun around on the spot, looking up at the crystal chandelier in the centre of the grand entrance. "Are they real diamonds?"

The old housekeeper grumbled under her breath, then disappeared into the depths of the house, leaving Julia and Jessie standing at the foot of the sweeping mahogany staircase. Through an open door to the kitchen, Julia could see caterers and waiters running around making final preparations for the garden party. It was all a little excessive for Julia's tastes, but it seemed like the right amount of extravagance for Katie Wellington-South.

Julia turned in time to see her dad ducking out of a room as he buttoned up his cufflinks. He didn't seem to have noticed her. She didn't doubt that he thought she was just another member of staff blending into the walls. When he spotted her, his eyes bulged as wide as the housekeeper's.

"Julia," he said, the surprise loud and clear in his voice. "You came."

Brian walked across the mahogany floorboards, his Cuban heels clicking with each step. His skin was tanned and weathered, nodding to his numerous holidays a year. Glistening oil slicked his greying, but still thick black hair off his face. Some of that hair prickled his broad chest, which could be seen through his open collar. It seemed to be open an extra button lower every time Julia saw him. A chunky gold watch, which she didn't doubt was twenty-four karat, hung from his wrist, and the cufflinks he was fiddling with looked to be solid diamonds. He looked just like the man Julia had come to know as her father, but nothing like the man who had worn comfortable jeans and moth-eaten jumpers she still held onto in the depths of her memories.

"I made a Victoria sponge cake," Julia said meekly, her cheeks burning scarlet.

"My favourite," he said, ducking in for a quick kiss on Julia's cheek, filling her nostrils with his overpowering musky aftershave. "You've always remembered that."

He accepted the cake tin and cast it onto a table, which was creaking under the weight of a vase overflowing with white lilies. Brian's eyes wandered over to Jessie, and it was obvious he was immediately judging her well-worn red Converse, ripped up skinny jeans and baggy jumper. The hairs on the back of Julia's neck stood defensively on end.

"This is Jessie," Julia offered before he asked. "She's been staying with me for a while."

"Like a lodger?" he asked, one of his dark brows darting up. "Is money tight? You know you only have to -,"

"She's also working in my café," Julia interrupted, not wanting to get onto the conversation of money. "Aren't you, Jessie?"

"Mmhmm. Was homeless before Julia took me in."

Lemonade and Lies

Julia enjoyed the shock in her father's eyes, but it also broke her heart. The man she was clinging onto in her mind wouldn't have looked at somebody in need like that.

"How is that little café of yours doing?" he asked, turning his attention back to Julia.

"It's doing fine. Very busy, in fact."

"I keep meaning to pop in," he said. "I'm always hearing good things."

Julia knew he wasn't going to '*pop in*', just as much as he did. Ever since she had returned to Peridale and told him that she was going to open a café, he had treated her dream with amusement, as if the whole thing was nothing more than a hobby to keep Julia occupied and distracted while her divorce raged in the background.

"This announcement must be something pretty big if you've invited the whole village up here," Julia said, eager to discover the truth.

"Any excuse for a garden party," he said with an uneasy laugh. "You know what Katie is like. I can't stop and chat. I promised her I would check on how things are going outside. Is your sister coming?"

"She's coming later with Gran."

"Mum's coming?" he said, his eyes glazing over a little. "Of course. I'll see you later. Jessie, it was nice to meet you."

"Yeah," Jessie said, her dark eyes narrowing to slits as her arms folded tightly across her chest. "So nice."

Brian hovered for a moment, his eyes briefly meeting Julia's. His heels let out a small squeak against the freshly polished wood as he turned and headed in the direction of the garden. When they were alone, Julia and Jessie looked at each other, neither of them seeming to know what to say.

"Well, he seems like a real old -,"

"Maybe coming here wasn't a good idea," Julia interrupted, cutting Jessie off before she let out an expletive. "Every time he sees me he looks like he's going to throw up."

"I noticed that too," Jessie agreed as she sucked the air in through her teeth. "Will there be food at this thing? I'm starving."

In the next hour the rest of the villagers arrived, including Julia's sister and gran. They mingled in the entrance hall sipping champagne and eating tiny canapés, which were being handed out by handsome men in tuxedos carrying silver trays.

"I wanted proper food," Jessie mumbled under her breath. "Not this posh finger stuff."

Lemonade and Lies

"I'd usually tell somebody your age not to be so ungrateful, but I'll agree with you there," Dot, Julia's gran, said as she nibbled at the edge of a canapé. "What is this?"

"Smoked salmon," Sue said, tossing one whole into her mouth. "I quite like it."

Dot shot Sue a sharp look as she pushed up her tightly wound curls at the back of her head. She peered around at the faces in the crowd looking as uncomfortable as Julia felt. If Julia felt like her relationship with her father was strained, it was nothing compared to her gran's.

"I didn't raise him this way," Dot muttered under her breath. "All of this excess is bad for the soul. It will rot him from the inside out."

"You know it's all *her*," Sue said, grabbing another smoked salmon canapé off a passing tray. "She's a *Wellington*."

"And he's a *South*!" Dot said, her lips pursing tightly. "Your grandfather would turn in his grave if he knew your father had married into this ghastly family. All of this for a silly announcement? It's beyond belief!"

Sue caught Julia's eyes, and for a moment, both of the sisters knew what the other was thinking. They quickly looked away, neither of them wanting to acknowledge the elephant in the room.

"I heard she was pregnant," said Emily Burns, who lived in the cottage next to Julia's. "It's been all around the village."

"I heard they were getting divorced," added Amy Clark, the village's organist at St. Peter's Church.

"Who has a party to announce a divorce?" Emily bit back. "That's preposterous. Mark my words, it's a baby! Evelyn from the B&B said so, and she has the sight, you know."

"A baby at his age?" Amy said, rolling her eyes. "Rubbish."

Julia caught Sue's eyes again, and it was only when she saw her own worry in her sister's eyes that she realised she had stopped breathing. She shook her head and let out a long breath, her cheeks flushing red. Dot and Jessie were both staring at her with worry in their eyes.

"Will you excuse me?" Julia said, already turning around. "Nature calls."

Before any of them could say anything, Julia pushed through the crowd and hurried up the mahogany staircase, and straight into the bathroom. She remembered where it was from her infrequent visits to the manor house. She slammed the heavy door into its frame and dragged the lock across. It nipped the skin on her left index finger. She cried out and crammed the bloody cut in her mouth, closing her eyes and trying to calm herself.

She walked over to the mirror hanging over the sink and assessed her reflection. Her cheeks were plump and naturally rosy, framing her delicate nose and wide green eyes. Her brows and lashes were dark and shapely, matching her dark curly hair in hue. She rarely wore makeup, but today she had opted for mascara and a little berry lipstick. It was the only thing stopping her from splashing cold water on her face.

Since she had read the invitation, she had only been able to think of one thing. It had been spinning around in her mind, tormenting her every waking thought. She had hoped she was overthinking things, but she saw the same worry in her sister's eyes. Hearing Emily say the words she had been afraid to say out loud made her stomach tighten.

Could her father be having another baby? She wanted to laugh at the suggestion, but she knew it was more than possible, what with Katie being the much younger one in the relationship. She had always wondered if this was where things were heading for her father and his new wife. It hadn't seemed like a possibility until yesterday.

She looked her reflection dead in the eyes and asked why she was so bothered if he was to have another baby. Her mind answered instantly, and much quicker than she had expected.

Julia was now the same age her mother had been when she had died. As a twelve-year-old girl, she hadn't realised just how young thirty-seven was, but as it looked back at her in the mirror, she knew she had so much life left in her. Her father had lived his life, and now that he was in his early-sixties, the thought of him bringing another life into the world, a possible brother or sister for Julia, sounded outrageous.

She immediately felt jealous of this invented younger sibling, who would no doubt benefit from her father's years of making mistakes. When her mother died, her father was physically there, but he wasn't mentally, leaving Julia and Sue's gran to pick up the pieces and raise the girls as if they were her own children.

Their father danced around the country dealing antiques, rarely visiting Peridale, and growing more and more distant from his daughters. He would bring them extraordinary gifts from his travels, but eventually they faded away. It hadn't taken Julia long to realise they were just a smoke screen for his lack of caregiving. With Sue being the younger daughter, it took longer for her bubble to burst, which explained why she was more defensive of his actions than Julia cared to be.

By the time he finally moved back to Peridale and settled, Julia was living in London and Sue was already married. He was a stranger to both of them, and their interactions had become nothing more than polite exchanges when they happened to see each other. He was a shadow of the caring and loving man Julia remembered from before her mother's death. She wondered if Sue even remembered that version of their father.

Turning her attention back to the present, Julia shook her curls out and acknowledged that the announcement could be one of many things. She washed her hands, dried them on a fluffy towel adorned with the Wellington family crest, and headed back to the door, her heels clicking on the exposed floorboards.

At the top of the grand staircase, she was surprised when she didn't hear the chatter of the party below. It seemed they had moved through to the garden without her. She didn't mind. It would give her a little longer to gather her thoughts. Just as she was about to descend the staircase, a raised man's voice ricocheted down the hallway, catching her attention. She turned to look in the direction of the voice, her foot hovering over the top step. It was coming from a slightly open door at the end of the hall. She listened to the raised voice, not quite able to make out what he was talking about. She would have left it, but she heard the distinct high-pitched squawk of Katie Wellington-South, and it sent a familiar shiver running down her spine.

Peridale village was renowned for its gossipers, and even though Julia rarely engaged in the gossiping, the intrigued villager within her itched to know what the shouting was about. Backing up the hallway, she slowly crept towards the open door.

"This has nothing to do with you!" Katie screamed, her shrill voice piercing through the air like nails down a chalkboard. "This is my decision!"

"This has everything to do with me!" the man cried back, matching her volume.

If Julia had recognised the man's voice as her father's, she would have promptly retreated because she didn't want to overhear something so private. As it happened, she didn't recognise the man, so she crept closer.

"You're always interfering!" Katie yelled.

Lemonade and Lies

"Always trying to ruin things for me. You're never happy unless I'm miserable."

"Miserable?" the man cried, laughing sarcastically. "You don't know the meaning of the word! You have everything! Dad has let you live in this house all your life, and yet I was tossed out at eighteen to be shown the harsh realities of the world. What did you do? You messed around with your stupid modelling career, and then when that didn't work, you ran back to Daddy and held your hand out. What did Dad do? He tossed every coin you could catch at you. And now *this*! Are you really that bored that this is what you want to do with your time?"

"I need something too, Charles!" Katie cried. "I'm stuck here all day, going out of my mind looking after Dad. He can barely get out of bed these days. Do you know how difficult it is for me?"

"Am I supposed to feel sorry for you?" Charles cried back. "Because I don't. I *never* will. You're still the spoiled little brat you always were. It never mattered that I was the oldest. You've always been his little princess, regardless of what you do. All you care about is getting your hands on my inheritance."

"That's not true!"

"So why are you doing this? This is all I'll have

when he's gone. This house was my ticket into the green. Do you know how difficult it is running my own business? People aren't buying like they used to, but you wouldn't know that. You're up here, playing with *his* millions, while I'm struggling to keep my own roof over my head."

The arguing stopped for a moment. Julia thought she was about to be outed. She heard footsteps heading towards the door, but they turned back as if someone was pacing. Reaching into her handbag, Julia pulled out a small compact mirror, and placed it against the edge of the open door. She fiddled with the angle for a second before she landed on Katie, and then on the man, who she was sure she recognised.

"The old man will never give me the house now," Charles said, shaking his head. "You've got him right where you want him."

"It's not like that, Charles."

"It's always like that with you, Katie," Charles said, before turning around, his eyes almost looking straight at Julia in the mirror. "You're no sister of mine."

Julia jumped back into the shadow of a doorway just in time. She stared into the mirror, pretending she was fixing her hair. Charles stopped and looked directly into her eyes, before shaking his head and running down the staircase, taking them two at a time.

Julia heard the click of Katie's impossibly high heels heading towards the door, so she ran as quickly as she dared back into the bathroom, resting her ear against the wood until she felt it safe to venture out. The last thing she wanted was for Katie to take her anger out on her, or even worse, try and engage her in a conversation.

When the coast was clear, Julia left the bathroom, made her way down the staircase and towards the garden, the knot in her stomach only growing tighter with each step. Everything she had heard from the Wellington siblings had only confirmed her suspicions about the '*big announcement*'.

CHAPTER 3

Julia joined Jessie, Sue and Dot in the garden. They were all sipping large glasses of freshly squeezed lemonade, which were being handed out on trays. Julia grabbed one and crammed the straw in her mouth, needing the sugar rush.

"Where have you been?" Dot asked, glancing around the crowded garden. "I was about to send out a search party. Everybody in the village is here!"

Lemonade and Lies

"I got lost," Julia lied, hoping that would wash.

Her gran arched a brow, letting her know it certainly didn't wash, but she didn't push it. Julia wondered if her gran could sense the worry in Julia's eyes, and she was just choosing not to acknowledge the baby shaped elephant in the room because she couldn't bear the thought of it being true.

"Detective Inspector Brown is over there," Sue whispered in Julia's ear after jabbing her in the ribs. "He's talking to psychic Evelyn."

"I wonder if he's asking her when you'll say yes to him asking you out on a date?" Dot added, standing on tiptoes to look over to where Barker was, as though she would be able to hear what he was talking to Evelyn about. "It's been nearly a month since he asked you. '*Maybe*' won't cut it forever, you know."

Julia's cheeks blushed. She took a long sip of the lemonade, which tasted as fresh as a summer's day. Barker caught her gaze across the crowd and sent a little wave in her direction. A smile took over her face as she sent a small wave back.

"Your face has gone all red," Jessie said unsubtly. "Are you feeling okay?"

"She's in *loooove*," Sue said, making sure to drag out the word for as long as possible.

"Give it a rest, will you?" Julia said, dropping her hair over her face. "I wouldn't exactly call it that."

Julia didn't know what she would call it. Barker had moved to the village just over a month ago, and his first week had been spent butting heads with Julia as she interfered with Gertrude Smith's suspicious murder case. When Julia figured out the murderer before Detective Inspector Brown had a chance to, he seemed to gain newfound respect for her, and he asked her out on a date. Julia's response had been '*maybe*', and even though she knew she did want to go on a date with the tall, dark and handsome Detective Inspector, saying '*yes*' hadn't seemed so easy.

"Good afternoon, ladies," Barker said as he approached them, clutching his own glass of lemonade. "Lovely day for it, don't you think?"

"Quite," Dot said. "How's the detecting going?"

"Trying to keep the village safe," Barker said, his charismatic smile beaming from ear to ear. "I've been trying to get this one to ditch the café and join the force after her turn at playing detective."

"Hear that, Julia?" Sue said, her brows darting up and down as her lips hovered over her straw. "Barker thinks you're good enough to go pro."

Lemonade and Lies

"I'm going to barf," Jessie mumbled under her breath after loudly sucking the last of her lemonade from her ice filled glass. "I'm going to get a refill."

"We'll come with," Dot said, grabbing Sue's arm and dragging her with Jessie. "Have fun, you two."

Julia smiled awkwardly as her family disappeared, leaving her alone with Barker. For a moment, they silently stood and observed the garden party unfolding around them. When they both seemed ready to talk, they turned, and tried to speak at the same time.

"Ladies first," Barker said, with a small laugh.

"I don't think detective work is for me," Julia said, her finger playing with the top of the green and white straw jutting out of a lemon wedge in her glass. "I'm much more suited to baking cakes."

"You do make a mean double chocolate fudge cake," Barker said, nodding in agreement. "But you also ran circles around me when it came to finding Gertrude Smith's killer."

Hearing that made Julia swell up with pride. Part of the reason she had been so invested in finding the murderer before Barker was because he suspected her friend, Roxy Carter, of committing the crime, and another part felt underestimated by Barker, and she wanted to prove herself.

"So how did you score yourself an invitation to this thing?" Julia asked, eager to shift the focus of the conversation.

"Katie dropped by the station with invitations for all the boys," Barker said, sipping his lemonade. "She seemed quite keen that I come."

"Katie?"

"Do you know her?"

Julia awkwardly sucked her lemonade, glancing around the crowd. She spotted Jessie, Sue and Dot all watching eagerly. Dot sent over two thumbs up, which Sue quickly dragged down and mouthed her apologies.

"She's married to my dad," Julia said bluntly.

Barker choked on his lemonade and stared down at her, eyes wide as the housekeeper's, and as amused as her father's. "Seriously? But she's so – *young*."

"You think?" Julia agreed, chewing the inside of her cheek.

"Doesn't that mean she's your step-,"

"Don't say it," Julia held her hand up. "I've had enough of that from Jessie."

They both laughed, and paused to suck their lemonade. Eager to change the subject again, Julia edged the topic to something more intriguing.

"Any interesting cases?" Julia asked.

Lemonade and Lies

"You know I can't talk about them," Barker said. "There is something I wanted to ask you, actually. Remember that night in your café when I asked you out on a -,"

Barker's sentence was stopped midway when a collective cry rippled through the crowd. Everybody turned at once to look for the epicentre, which became very apparent, very quickly. Two men appeared to be brawling in the middle of the crowd, causing people to edge forward to form a circle around the fight. Peridale could pretend to be as civilised as the next village, but Julia knew the second something exciting was happening, no matter how low-brow, everyone wanted to be able to give their own eyewitness account.

"Out of the way!" Barker cried. "I'm police!"

That threat alone parted the sea of people. Julia took advantage of the parting and stuck close to Barker, her own curiosity getting the better of her. They both broke out into the clearing, where one man had another pinned to the ground. Julia instantly recognised both of the struggling men. The man writhing in the grass was Charles Wellington, the brother who had been arguing with Katie not so long ago. The man on top was Richard May, a local man who Julia was trying to create a cinnamon, rose and orange wedding cake for.

"How could you?" Richard cried out, his fist ready to strike Charles' face. "You're a little swine! I'm going to have you!"

"We'll have less of that," Barker called out, scooping Richard off Charles as if he weighed no more than a bag of flour. "Calm down! There are children here."

For a moment, the red mist didn't fade from Richard's eyes, until he looked around and saw the sea of scared and confused faces. He pushed his long, messy hair out of his red face, then tore free of Barker's grip. He doubled back through the crowd and disappeared.

"What was all that about?" Dot whispered in Julia's ear, appearing from nowhere. "Who's that on the ground? I know that face."

"Katie's brother," Julia mumbled, almost without realising. "I remember him from the wedding."

"Oh yeah," Sue said, also appearing from nowhere. "He got drunk during the reception and started swearing at Katie. My Neil was one of the men who had to drag him out."

Barker held out a hand for Charles, but it was ignored. Charles stumbled up to his feet, and tossed his hands defensively over his head, casting his sharp eyes around the crowd of waiting faces.

"What are you all looking at?" Charles screamed out, with the same anger Julia had heard earlier. "*Huh?*"

People jumped back as if he were a rabid animal ready to attack, even though he had been the one being attacked by Richard. Charles smoothed out his icy blonde hair, and pushed his way through the crowd, disappearing into the house.

"What could have gotten into Richard like that?" somebody in the crowd mused.

"I heard he was having trouble with Sally," another said. "Right before the wedding, too."

"I'm supposed to be making their wedding cake," Julia thought aloud.

The chatter wore on along with the afternoon. Just when Julia finished her third sickly sweet glass of lemonade, and thought the point of the garden party had long since been lost, a long nail tapping on a microphone echoed through the crowd.

"Who in the world is *that*?" Jessie asked, barely able to contain her laughter.

"That's Katie Wellington-South," Julia said.

Jessie looked from Julia, then back to the

woman teetering along the stage in platform shoes as she continued to tap her red nail on the microphone.

"You're kidding me?" Jessie said. "*That's* your step-mum?"

"She's not our step-mum," Sue jumped in. "And we wish we were kidding."

They all stared at Katie, whose platinum blonde hair had been blow dried into a curly mane, thicker and longer than naturally possible. Her makeup, as usual, was bright and could be seen right at the back of the crowd. Her shirt was typically tight, cutting off above her pierced navel, and straining over her ample and artificially enhanced bosom, which sat abnormally high under her chin. As she opened her plump, glossy lips to smile, her impeccably white teeth gleamed out, brighter than the sun in the cloudless sky. A couple of people seemed shocked by the woman's appearance, but most of Peridale already knew Katie Wellington-South and her ways.

"Is this thing on?" she mumbled, her squeaky voice causing static across the airwaves. "Brian, am I transmitting?"

Brian, who was standing just off to the side of the stage gave Katie two enthusiastic thumbs up. He was standing behind a wheelchair, which contained a barely conscious Vincent Wellington, who was hardly recognisable behind his oxygen mask. Julia knew he wasn't much older than Dot, but he seemed twice as old as any person she had ever met.

"Welcome, one and all," Katie squealed, casting her beaming clown-like grin at the audience, shielding her eyes from the sun. "Can you all hear me in the back?"

There was a mumble and nodding of heads as everybody peered to the back of the crowd. Julia noticed the same perplexed and entertained looks in people's eyes.

"Thank you all for coming here on such short notice," Katie squealed, not seeming to realise the purpose of a microphone. "I hope you've all been enjoying the canapés and our special Wellington family lemonade recipe, passed down from my great-great-grandmother, Bertha Wellington."

The woman in front of Julia let out an audible yawn. The man beside her checked his watch. Just like Julia, they hadn't come for a history lesson, they had come to find out the mystery behind the announcement.

"I'm sure you're all wondering why you are here today," Katie said. "It's because my husband and I have some *very* exciting news to share with you all. Isn't that right, Brian? Why don't you come up here?"

Katie motioned for Brian to join her. He shook his head and held his hands up. Katie didn't seem to get the hint, so she teetered over to the stairs at the side of the small stage and dragged him up. He waved awkwardly into the crowd as they walked across the stage together. One person tried to start a slow round of applause; it didn't catch.

"Hello everyone," Brian mumbled into the microphone Katie had crammed in front of his mouth. "Thanks for coming up here today."

Katie wrapped her arm around his waist, and Brian did the same. Their age gap was never more apparent than when they were standing side-by-side.

"How old *is* she?" Jessie mumbled, still clearly shocked.

"She's the same age as me," Julia said as coolly as she could. "She's thirty-seven and he – *my father* – he is sixty-two."

Jessie's eyes shot open, and her hand clamped over her mouth to contain the laughter. Julia was glad their age gap amused her, because all it did for Julia was turn her stomach. She would never forget the day she found out over the phone from her gran that her father was marrying a woman the same age as her. At first she had thought it was one of her gran's twisted jokes, but she wasn't that lucky.

"So, our big announcement," Katie said, letting out a small squeal of excitement. "We're very pleased – *no*, not pleased. What's the right word, baby?"

"I'm going to throw up," Sue mumbled. "This is unbearable."

"We're over the moon?" Brian offered, looking a lot more uncomfortable than Katie did with the microphone in his face.

"*Yes!*" Katie agreed. "We're *over* the moon to announce that we are turning Peridale Manor into a luxury spa!"

Katie squawked and bounced up and down on her dreadfully high heels, looking out expectantly into the crowd. Julia turned to Sue, both frowning at one another. Julia wiggled her finger in her ear, wondering if she had heard that right.

"Is that it?" Dot rolled her eyes, passing her lemonade to Julia. "Hold this. I've been clinging onto my bladder since she got up onto the stage. Fill me in on what I miss."

Dot trundled through the crowd and back into the house. Julia and Sue both turned back to the stage, where Katie had stopped bouncing, and was staring disappointedly into the sea of puzzled faces.

"Not the reaction I was expecting," she

mumbled quietly into the microphone. "Let me say it again. We're turning Peridale Manor into a luxury spa!"

"We heard you the first time!" a man heckled from the crowd.

"You called us up here for *that*?" a woman cried. "We thought you were *pregnant*!"

"Pregnant?" Katie laughed, her hand dancing over her exposed midriff. "God, no. With this figure? *No*. My husband and I, with the permission of my father, are turning this great manor into a spa. We'll offer luxury beauty treatments and weekend packages for the ultimate relaxation experience!"

Katie stared into the crowd again, but she seemed to be angering people more with each word that left her glossy lips. Julia didn't care what else happened, she was just glad her pregnancy fears had been her imagination playing tricks on her.

"How are we supposed to afford that?" Amy Clark, the elderly organist, called. "We're regular folk with regular jobs in these parts."

"Well, people will come from out of town to stay here for the weekend," Katie said, a small awkward laugh escaping her lips. "It's a *good* thing! Think about how all of the businesses in town will benefit from the extra tourism."

"It'll attract rich *yuppies!*" the same man from earlier cried. "They'll treat our village like their playground!"

Katie opened her mouth, but nothing came out. The crowd was growing more restless with every passing second. She dropped the microphone to her side, and started whispering into Brian's ear. He whispered something back, and she nodded. She clicked her fingers at a tuxedo-wearing waiter who was hovering by the side of the stage. He hurried over, crammed a hard hat over Katie's enormous hair, a heavy fluorescent jacket over her revealing outfit, and helped her switch from her platform stilettos to heavy work boots.

Now that the free food and lemonade had dried up, the chattering in the crowd grew louder and louder. People seemed less happy to stand around listening to Katie talk now that the cat was out of the bag. Katie looked out from under her yellow hardhat and lifted the microphone up to her lips again, seeming to sense the unrest.

"If you would all like to follow me in an orderly fashion, I'd like to show you the construction on our brand new outdoor pool, which will be open to all Peridale residents free of charge during the week."

The mumbling died down a little. The sound of

a free swimming pool seemed to ease the villagers.

"What about weekends?" somebody cried.

"Well, of course there will be a *small* charge at the weekends. Now, if you would all like to follow me."

A couple of people started to boo the charade, but Katie was either choosing not to listen, or she couldn't hear it under the heavy hardhat. She started walking towards the steps, assisted by Brian, who was carrying her shoes like a butler. Before she reached the edge of the stage, an invader snatched the microphone out of her hand and took the spot where she had been standing. The crowd suddenly grew silent.

"You hear *that*, little sister?" Charles called out through the microphone. "The people of Peridale don't *want* your spa. They don't *want* you to turn this *great* manor into a circus."

For the first time all day, there was a cheer. Some people were even clapping. It seemed they had short memories and couldn't remember the same man fighting on the ground not too long ago.

"This manor is a *symbol* of this town and it *shouldn't* be touched. Who's with me?"

Charles turned the microphone into the crowd, and a rapturous cheer crackled through the large speakers. Julia assessed Charles with caution. The argument she had heard earlier suddenly made more sense, and she was sure the intention behind Charles' sudden bout of village pride wasn't inspired by historical preservation.

"You ruin *everything!*" Katie screeched, her shrill voice traveling throughout the grounds without the aid of a microphone.

"This house will become a spa over my dead body," Charles said firmly, before dropping the microphone and pushing his way off the stage.

The entire crowd moved towards Charles, hoping to catch a glimpse of his next actions. He disappeared around the side of the house, quickly followed by a crying and shrieking Katie, and Brian, who tried to calm his wife. Vincent was still sitting by the side of the stage, staring into space. He didn't seem to have a clue where he was or what was going on.

"Your family is nuts!" Jessie exclaimed excitedly. "What was all that about?"

Julia almost mentioned the argument she had eavesdropped upon earlier, but decided against it. There were too many pairs of ears listening for a scrap of real gossip to explain what had just happened.

"Should we go after them?" Sue asked, standing on tiptoes to look over the crowd.

"Let's leave them," Julia said, resting a hand on Sue's shoulders, pushing her back into the grass. "They'll sort it out."

Out of nowhere, a dozen men carrying trays filled with more canapés and lemonade dispersed through the crowd. The rumbling calmed, and the free food and drinks went down a treat. Even Julia was growing to like the taste of the Wellington family lemonade. She thought she sensed a dash of grapefruit mixed in with the lemons and sugar, and made a mental note to try such a mix in a cake.

"A spa in Peridale?" Barker said as he made his way over to Julia. "I'm not so against the idea myself. I like a massage as much as the next man."

"You city folk," Sue said, rolling her eyes. "Full of your airs and graces. I wouldn't mind the free pool though. I hate having to drive out of the village in the summer when I want an outdoor swim."

"What do you think, Julia?" Jessie asked. "For or against your nutty step-mum's spa?"

Before Julia could correct Jessie about her use of the word '*step-mum*', the crack of shattering glass pierced through the air, silencing everything. It just so happened that Julia was facing the right way to see a man bursting through an upstairs window of the manor house, surrounded by a flurry of glass shards. He travelled noiselessly to the ground, his arms floating above his body, but not reaching out for air as Julia expected a man falling from a second story window would.

Julia heard the thud of his body hit the grass. She was in no doubt that the man was dead. Suddenly realising who the man could be, she dropped her lemonade and pushed through the crowd, not needing Barker's police credentials to do the work for her.

With Sue hot on her heels, she burst through the ring of shocked faces that had gathered around the face down man in the grass. When Julia saw the icy blonde of Charles Wellington's hair, she instantly felt guilty for feeling relieved that it wasn't her father.

"What have I missed?" Julia heard her gran call through the crowd. "What are you all huddled over for?"

CHAPTER 4

J ulia looked up at the broken window, along with many others, all seeming to want to find a clue worthy of gossiping about. The only remnants of the window were tiny, jagged shards around the perimeter of the frame. Charles had fallen through the window with some considerable force.

"He's dead," Barker whispered quietly as he checked the man's pulse. "Julia, can you call for an ambulance?"

Julia scrambled for her phone, her heart pounding in her chest. Pushing the phone into her ear, she turned to see the shock on her gran's face as Sue told her what had happened. Jessie was staring down at the body, her mouth opening and closing like a fish out of water.

Minutes later, an ambulance and two police cars were speeding towards Peridale Manor while Detective Inspector Brown attempted to clear the scene. In a village where everybody needed to know everything about everyone, it was a task easier said than done.

"What's everyone crowding around for?" Julia heard Katie's shrill shriek call across the garden. "Will somebody *answer* me?"

People dropped their heads and guiltily backed away from the body on the ground. A path cleared for Katie to stumble forward, still in her heavy work boots, jacket, and yellow safety helmet. She saw the limp body of her brother on the ground, and her wide eyes scanned the crowd as tears gathered along her heavily coated lashes.

"*No!*" she whimpered, burying her head in Brian's chest as inky mascara streaked down her rouged cheeks. "*No!*"

Brian stared ahead at the body, his eyes wide and unblinking as he comforted his sobbing wife. As her pained screeches grew louder, the thinner the crowd around the body became.

The uniformed officers got to work securing the scene and successfully brushing away the remaining villagers. Julia, her gran, Sue and Jessie all hung back, and it was obvious none of them knew if they should also leave. Julia heard her gran mutter something about being related when an officer approached them, which seemed to give her a pass to stay and stare. Julia on the other hand had something more important to do when she caught Barker slipping away from the madness and into the house.

"I need the bathroom," Julia whispered to Sue as she slipped away.

Taking the mahogany staircase as carefully as she could, she crept up them for the second time that day. When she reached the top step, she spotted Barker at the end of the hallway, crouched under the broken window. The noise from the garden fluttered through the curtains of the empty frame.

"I'd say he was pushed," Julia said as she approached Barker. "Quite hard too, if you ask me. Knocked the entire window out of its frame."

"You know you can't be up here, Julia," Barker mumbled as he inspected a stray shard of glass that had fallen inwards. "It's a crime scene."

"I won't touch anything."

Julia crept forward, scanning the hallway for anything out of the ordinary. The lavishly decorated walls were lined with ornate landscape paintings in heavy gold frames. Ornaments on tall stands sat under the paintings, illuminated by sconces jutting out of the walls.

"This stand is empty," she thought aloud, summoning Barker up from the ground. "If you look, there are three display stands on each side of the wall, between the window and these two doors, all containing an ornament, but this one is empty."

Barker looked from a vase to an ornate figure of a glass ballerina on the two stands on either side of the empty one, but Julia's frustration started to bubble when she noticed familiar dismissal in his eyes.

"That's hardly a clue, Julia," Barker said, turning his attention back to the window. "Who says there was anything on that plinth?"

Julia stared down at the empty stand, noticing a definite wobbly line in the centre, indicating that something had been there. She crouched down so that she was eye-level with the stand, and under the bright light, there was an unmistakable layer of dust everywhere, apart from the centre where whatever had been taken had stood.

Julia pulled out her phone and snapped a quick picture of the shape etched in the dust while Barker's back was turned.

"I'm calling this a crime scene, so you need to leave."

"Yes, sir. Good luck with the investigation."

"You've got that look in your eyes again," Barker moaned. "Please, Julia, I *implore* you to leave this one to me."

"What is this look people keep talking about?"

"It's the same look you had when you were trying to outsmart me by finding Gertrude Smith's murderer before I did."

Julia concealed her smile as she turned on her heels, not wanting to remind Barker that she had outsmarted the Detective Inspector by finding the murderer before he had.

As she walked along the hallway and back towards the staircase, she looked down at the floor, the nervous bubbling in her stomach growing louder each time she spoke to Barker. She was sure he was about to re-ask her out on that date in the garden before Charles and Richard's fight, and this time she was sure she would have said yes. While she looked down, she spotted muddy boot prints barely visible on the oak floorboards. Glancing over her shoulder, she concentrated on the floor as Barker spoke on the phone. The boot prints ran all the way down the hall, stopping just before the window. They then trailed back into the bathroom where Julia had hidden earlier. The door was open so she glanced inside, noting that the boot prints suddenly vanished in front of the bathtub, almost as if somebody had sat on the edge of the bath and removed their boots.

Julia thought about attracting Barker to the boot prints, but he had told her to stay out of his investigation. If he were worth his Detective Inspector badge, he would notice the faint footprints and come to his own conclusions. Julia decided she would let Barker get on with his investigation, but that didn't mean she wouldn't get on with her own. She pulled her recipe notepad out of her bag, flipped past a page of ingredients for a new chocolate orange scone she wanted to try, and scribbled down everything she had just learned.

Back in the garden, Julia re-joined her gran, Sue and Jessie just at the very moment a stretcher covered in a red blanket was hoisted into the back of an ambulance.

On the edge of the stage, Katie was still sobbing into Brian's arms, while Brian watched the stretcher, still unblinking. Vincent Wellington gawked at the grass from behind his oxygen mask, unaware of what had just happened to his son.

"If I get like that, I want you girls to put me out of my misery," Dot said when she noticed Julia looking at the wheelchair-bound old man. "Take me out to a farm, and put a bullet in my back. I won't stop you."

"*Gran*!" Sue whispered, slapping Dot's arm with the back of her hand. "A man has *just* died!"

"I'm just saying!" Dot protested, rubbing the spot where Sue had just tapped her. "That's no life. I'm not surprised he agreed to let Katie turn this place into a spa. She probably asked over dinner while a nurse dribbled soup down his chin. Poor man wouldn't have had a clue what he was agreeing to."

When Dot finished talking, neither Julia nor Sue spoke. Instead, they looked uncomfortably at each other, both hearing truth in their gran's statement, but also not wanting to give her permission to keep ranting at the scene of a man's murder.

"Should we say something?" Sue whispered to Julia, as they both looked over to their father. "Poor man looks in shock."

"I think we should leave it," Julia whispered back.

"He's still our father, Julia."

Julia's heart twitched in her chest. She knew that was true, but the unblinking coldness of his eyes had shaken her to her very core. It was the exact same look that had taken over him when Julia's mother had been lowered in the ground all those years ago. Sue probably didn't remember, but it was etched in Julia's memory like a red-hot stamp on a cow's backside. She particularly remembered how he had spent the entire day wordlessly staring into the distance, ignoring his two distraught daughters.

They watched on as officers wrapped crime scene tape around the spot where Charles Wellington had been. Julia knew it wouldn't be long before the forensics team turned up to document every detail of the scene. For now at least, there was nothing to be gained from lingering around at Peridale Manor.

After driving back into the village, Julia and Jessie parted ways from Dot and Sue, heading back up the winding lane leading to Julia's cottage. When they were alone, Julia noticed a similar vacantness in Jessie's eyes. It hadn't gone unnoticed that she hadn't said a word since the garden party had turned sour. Julia had just been waiting until they were alone before attempting to talk to her young lodger.

"I'm sorry you had to see that," Julia whispered, nudging Jessie softly with her arm. "It's never easy seeing your first dead body."

"That's not my first," Jessie said with a shrug, facing away from Julia.

"Oh. Right."

Julia was rendered speechless by the lack of emotion in Jessie's voice. She knew people could become detached when talking about death, but Julia hadn't expected somebody so young to be so weathered towards it. She wondered if she should push the subject, but like talking about Jessie's time on the streets, Julia knew it was probably best to wait for Jessie to voluntarily open up than pry for information.

"If you ever want to talk, I'm here," Julia offered, pulling her house keys out of her handbag as they climbed out of Julia's vintage aqua blue Ford Anglia.

Jessie didn't say anything, instead choosing to

nod as she chewed the inside of her lip. Julia unhooked her peeling white garden gate. As they walked towards her old cottage with its low thatched roof, she decided they were going to spend the afternoon baking, if only to keep both of their minds occupied.

CHAPTER 5

Monday morning in Julia's café was usually the quietest time of the week. It was when she spent her time deep cleaning the kitchen, and checking which ingredients were starting to run low. On the Monday morning following Charles Wellington's death, it became very apparent that her deep clean and stock check would have to wait.

Lemonade and Lies

For as long as Julia had owned the café, this was the first Monday morning in Julia's memory that there was a small cluster of residents waiting as she pulled her Ford Anglia into her small parking space. At first, Julia had thought the villagers just wanted to use her café as a base to hear all of the latest gossip regarding the recent death, but it turned out they had created a connection between Julia and Charles and they intended on using it.

"Has your father said anything yet?"

"How is your father doing?"

"I'm so sorry for your loss, Julia. Your family must be going through such a difficult time."

"Were you close to Charles?"

"How's Katie holding up? Poor woman having to see her brother like that."

By lunchtime, Julia was tired of repeating over and over that she knew no more than anyone else because she wasn't close to her father, and she had only met Charles once previously at her father's wedding. For most people, this didn't settle their insatiable thirst for more information, so they continued to quiz her regardless, certain she must be hiding something.

"Has your father called?" Dot asked, after hurrying in a little after one, her hands filled with bags of shopping. "He hasn't called me. The *cheek* of the man!"

"Why would he have called?" Julia poured Dot a cup of tea. "I doubt he even has my number."

"He's your *father*! You *deserve* to know what's going on," Dot said, dumping her bags at the table nearest the counter, which was where people usually sat when they wanted to talk with Julia as she worked. "I haven't heard a thing since yesterday! Everyone is talking, but nobody knows a thing."

Julia set the cup of tea in front of her gran, along with a bowl of sugar cubes, and a small jug of milk. Dot dumped four lumps of sugar and half of the milk into her tea, once again defying the doctor's warning of age-related Type 2 diabetes.

"I bet it was Richard," Dot exclaimed suddenly after taking a deep sip of her hot tea, the cup barely pulled away from her lips. "It *has* to be! We all saw that fight between him and Charles right before he was pushed to his death."

"But why would Richard May want to kill Charles?" asked Roxy Carter, who was in the café on her lunch break from the local primary school. "You can't accuse people of murder without any proof."

"What more proof do you need?" Dot cried, stamping her finger down on the table. "You *saw*

Richard trying to bash Charles' face in, didn't you?"

"I heard him and Sally had called their wedding off," Roxy said, taking a bite of one of Julia's brownies. "Maybe Richard was just taking his frustration out on the wrong person?"

"Or *maybe* he was getting ready to murder him!" Dot insisted. "Mark my words, young girl. The truth *will* come out with the dirty laundry."

Roxy's face turned a deep shade of red as she stared down at her brownie. Julia wasn't sure if her gran knew what she had just said, but the hurt was written all over Roxy's face. It hadn't been long since Roxy's romantic relationship with her teaching assistant, Violet, had been used to blackmail her by Gertrude Smith, thus putting her in the frame when Gertrude was murdered. Julia loved her gran, but along with the rest of Peridale, her first reaction was often an overreaction. It wouldn't be long until her gran's declaration of Richard's guilt spread around the village as fact, as it had done with an innocent Roxy.

After closing the café at the end of a long day, Julia sent Jessie back to the cottage with the house keys, leaving her to drive up to Peridale Manor alone with a beef casserole secured in the passenger seat. Pulling up alongside a lone police car, she secured her handbrake, casting an eye to her casserole, which she hoped would serve a dual purpose.

Julia unbuckled her seatbelt and pulled her keys out of the ignition. She opened her small black handbag, pulled out her small ingredients notepad, immediately flicking to the notes she had made. She had written a long list of things she wanted to find out. The first point, which she had circled multiple times, was to talk to Katie and her father.

Julia knew they would be too distraught to think about food, so she had baked a casserole out of concern, but she also hoped it was a valid excuse for visiting uninvited.

"Yes?" the surly housekeeper grumbled through a crack in the door after Julia rang the doorbell. "The Wellingtons aren't taking visitors."

Julia applied her kindest smile and pushed forward the casserole. The dumpy woman with the heavily lined eyes and pulled back wiry hair sourly looked Julia up and down.

"I was here yesterday," Julia offered.

"So was half the village, sweetheart," the woman snapped, her bulging eyes rolling. "Clear off."

"I'm Brian's daughter," Julia said, wondering if the housekeeper really didn't remember their meeting yesterday.

"Oh," the woman said with a heavy sigh, opening the door and stepping to the side. "I remember. You brought that insolent child with you."

Julia bit her tongue, knowing the venomous housekeeper could easily deny her entry if she wanted to. Taking her chance, she stepped over the threshold and into the grand entrance hall.

"I didn't catch your name yesterday," Julia said.

"That's because I didn't give it. I'll fetch Mr. South for you. Stay here."

The housekeeper shuffled away and headed towards the staircase, looking over her shoulder at Julia as she went. Julia smiled at her, which only seemed to anger the woman more. When she reached the top of the staircase and turned along the hall, Julia let out the breath she had been holding in, and took a couple of steps forward. She wondered what could have happened to the housekeeper to make her so bitter.

Julia placed the casserole on the lily filled table. The tin containing her Victoria sponge cake was still there, seemingly untouched from the previous day. Julia walked along the entrance hall towards the open door of the kitchen. Through the large windows above the stove, people moved back and forth. At first, she thought they were police officers, until she realised they were builders.

"Julia?" Katie called from the top of the staircase, the surprise loud and clear in her voice. "What are you doing here?"

Julia turned on her heels and scooped up the casserole dish as Katie made her way down the stairs. Julia hadn't expected to see Katie. She had assumed she was going to be curled up in bed, grief-stricken and distraught after her brother's death. Instead, she was as put together as always, her makeup thick and her hair voluminous. She was wearing all black, perhaps as an outwardly sign of mourning, but her stomach and chest were still poking through the sparse material.

"I made you a casserole. I didn't think you would want to be cooking today."

Katie stared down at the gravy and beef mixture through the plastic wrap, her lips pursed into what was obviously a fake smile.

"You know we've got our housekeeper, Hilary, for that," Katie said, awkwardly accepting the dish. "I'm sure your father will enjoy this. I don't eat meat on Mondays."

"Oh," Julia said, narrowing her eyes at the

strange woman who was the same age as Julia but different in every possible way. "I was hoping to speak to my father. Is he around?"

"He's at the station," Katie said as she walked through to the large and immaculate kitchen. "He's making a statement."

"A statement?" Julia asked, hurrying after Katie. "At the station?"

"I didn't want more police up here," Katie said as she pulled open the giant double doors of her fridge before balancing the casserole on wrapped trays of leftover canapés from the garden party. "The sooner things get back to normal, the better. Can I get you a drink? Perhaps some lemonade? There's plenty left over."

"That would be lovely," Julia said, not really wanting to sit and chat with Katie, but knowing it would give her a reason to stick around and find out what she wanted to know. "It really is good lemonade."

"Thank you," Katie said, a grin spreading from ear to ear as she rested a hand on her chest. Julia was amused to see a small streak of lipstick on Katie's teeth. "Do you really mean that?"

Julia nodded. Katie looked on the verge of tears for a moment, but she shook out her white blonde hair, and pulled a huge jug of the lemonade from the fridge. She poured two large glasses before sitting across from Julia, facing away from construction in the garden. As Katie busied herself stirring the lemon wedges and ice with her straw, Julia peered through the window and watched a team of workmen dig out what she suspected was going to be the pool Katie had wanted to show her unimpressed guests.

"I see work is still going ahead."

"No time like the present," Katie said, staring blankly, and yet somehow deeply into Julia's eyes. "There is lots of work to get done. The pool is just the start. We're converting the spare bedrooms into luxury guestrooms, each with their own bathroom. It was murder trying to get planning permission for all of this, but my father called in some favours from the council."

"It all seems rather grand," Julia said, trying to fake interest. "You must have been thinking about this for a long time."

"It's always been a dream of mine," Katie said. "Like that little café of yours."

Julia gritted her teeth and smiled. She could tell Katie viewed her café the same way her father did. Using what was left over from her lifesavings after buying her cottage hadn't been an easy decision.

Lemonade and Lies

Julia had known there was every chance her venture would fail, and she would be left broke with no income. Luckily, her cakes had hit the spot with the villagers, unlike Katie's idea for a spa. Julia looked at the wealthy woman examining her nails as if they were the most important things in the world. Julia wondered if she had ever had to worry about anything serious in her entire life.

"Any idea what time my father will be back?"

"No," Katie said, glancing to the giant station clock on the wall. "He's been there since this morning."

Julia glanced at the clock. It was nearly six in the evening. The police weren't taking a statement from her father; they were interrogating him.

"Where was my father when – when *it* happened?" Julia asked, her finger circling the lemonade glass.

Katie's expression tightened, as did her eyes. The caked on makeup creased into her fine lines, revealing her true age. Julia was glad she had lived a life without the shackles of makeup because she was sure it had allowed her to age a little more naturally.

"He was with me. After my brother ruined everything, we came inside to find him. We couldn't find him, so we went into Brian's study. He gave me some whiskey to calm my nerves. When I'd calmed down, we came out and – and saw *him*."

Julia thought for a moment that Katie was about to crack and start shrieking again, but she composed herself, showing more self-restraint than Julia had previously thought the vapid woman possessed.

"Did anybody see you together?"

"You sound like the police!" Katie said, her shrill voice suddenly rising at a rate that made Julia's arm hairs jump up. "Me and Brian were together. Now, if you *don't* mind, my father needs his medication. Hilary will show you out."

Julia hadn't realised Hilary was standing in the doorway, waiting to usher Julia out of the manor. She practically dragged Julia away from her lemonade, and tossed her outside. Standing in between the police car and her own vintage automobile, she pulled her notepad out of her bag, considering tearing out the notes she had made, so she could go home and forget about the whole thing. She ran her finger along the points she had made, pausing at '*Establish Katie and Dad's alibi*'. Julia pulled out her small metal pen and twisted out the nib to draw a big question mark over the word '*alibi*'. If she hadn't learned that her father had been at the station all day, she might have believed Katie's story about drinking whiskey in the study, but something wasn't sitting right with Julia.

Instead of walking towards her car, she cast an eye back at the manor, and when she was satisfied that she wasn't being watched, she crept around the side of the house, past the crime scene. A white tent had been erected and was being guarded by a lone officer. Julia sent a smile in his direction, but he didn't send one back. Walking past the crime scene, she made her way beyond the stage, which was still there from the day before, and towards the construction site she had seen through the kitchen window. She knew Katie would easily spot the yellow polka dots on her navy blue dress if she looked out, so Julia knew her time to investigate was limited.

"*Julia?*" a familiar voice called to her across the construction sight. "Julia, over here."

Julia looked past the construction workers to see Joanne Lewis standing by a car. Joanne worked in the village's charity shop, making her a regular in Julia's café. She was a tall, slender woman in her early-forties, with an elongated face and high forehead. Her tightly wound brown curls had been cut just above her jawline, making her face look even longer. Julia had always thought her hair would complement her face more if she let it grow out a little, but she was too kind to point that out.

"Joanne, what are you doing here?" Julia asked after weaving her way through the construction workers, who appeared to be packing up for the day as the blue sky turned pink.

"My Terry got the contract for this spa job," Joanne said, casting an eye over to the manor.

Julia looked over to the builders, instantly spotting Terry's bald head and potbelly hanging over his faded jeans. He was reading something from a clipboard on the steps of a builder's cabin. When Julia had first moved to the village, she had called on Terry's building expertise to help fit the kitchen and counter in her café. Terry had heavily discounted the work because Julia was a local, and she had thought favourably of him since.

"I didn't see you at the garden party yesterday," Julia said.

"I was back here with the boys. We were expecting Katie to bring the crowd around to see the progress on the digging, but – well, you know what happened next. We were waiting when we heard the glass shatter."

They both smiled awkwardly at each other, neither appearing to want to talk about the death.

Lemonade and Lies

Julia was sure this was the first villager she had encountered all day who didn't want to gossip, and she was glad of it.

"I'm sure Terry is pleased to get such a big contract," Julia said, wanting to fill the sudden awkwardness.

"He's managing the whole project," Joanne said proudly, her face lighting up. "It couldn't have come at a better time."

Before Julia could ask why the timing was good, Joanne's teenage son, Jamie Lewis, walked towards them, covered in mud and wearing a yellow hardhat.

"Hello, Jamie," Julia said, smiling at the teenager. "I didn't realise you had finished with school already."

"Dropped out," he said with a shrug, followed by a heavy yawn as he got into the car without saying another word.

Julia looked to Joanne who was maintaining her smile, even if it did look uncomfortable and strained.

"He was always going to end up in the family trade," Joanne offered, her tone sounding like an excuse, rather than an explanation. "He was never really good at exams, so we spoke to the school. They agreed to let him leave with our permission to

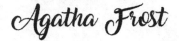

start his building apprenticeship early. He'll get a qualification from it in the end. I hear you've taken in a young girl off the streets?"

Julia sensed the urgency in Joanne's voice to quickly divert the topic of conversation away from her family. Julia hadn't told many people about what she had done for Jessie, but word had somehow still spread all over the village, and everybody seemed to have their own opinions on the situation, and they weren't shy about telling Julia about them.

"She's a good girl," Julia said. "Same age as your Jamie I think."

They both looked into the car as Jamie tapped away with his thumbs on his phone. In a way, he reminded Julia of Jessie. She wondered if all kids that age were allergic to talking.

"You should get her on an apprenticeship at the local college," Joanne suggested. "They help out with their wages, and you get them trained up. I'm sure I saw a baking apprenticeship in the prospectus. I'll drop it around to yours if you like?"

"That would be kind of you," Julia said. "Thank you."

"Are you adopting Jessie?" Joanne asked, still obviously wanting to keep the focus on Julia rather than herself. "I heard you were."

Lemonade and Lies

"You did?" Julia asked, wondering why she was surprised that false information had somehow spread around the village without her knowing about it. "I've spoken to her social worker, but I'm waiting on a letter about the next steps."

"It's a big responsibility taking on a troubled kid," Joanne said, pulling her car keys out of her pocket as Terry walked towards them, also covered in mud. "I better go. I've got a stew on a low light back home. I'll drop that college prospectus off sometime this week?"

"Thank you," Julia said, stepping away from the car.

She smiled at Terry Lewis, but he blanked her completely and jumped into the car. Julia wondered if she had misjudged the man.

Joanne gave Julia a little wave as she ducked into the car. Julia waved back, peering through the windows as Terry and Jamie both tapped silently away on their phones, the mirror image of each other. Julia's day had been long and exhausting, but she couldn't imagine how difficult a day of digging was on the mind and body.

As she drove through the darkening village, she was far too tired to think of anything related to Charles

Wellington. Her mind was securely fixed on a cup of peppermint and liquorice tea, a bubble bath, and a good book.

CHAPTER 6

J ulia woke to her alarm, groaning as she rolled over, wishing she could have another hour in bed. Jessie had woken her again with the sleepwalking in the early hours of the morning, but after she had stopped Jessie climbing into the shower in her night clothes, she crawled back into her own bed and fell straight back to sleep.

Over breakfast that morning, neither of them

spoke much, and Julia wondered if Jessie knew about her sleepwalking. Either way, Jessie didn't mention it, so Julia didn't push it.

When they arrived at the café, Julia was glad to see there wasn't a gossiping crowd waiting for her to open up. She left Jessie in charge of the counter and started on her deep clean, which would give her time to think, away from the few customers.

Unluckily for Julia, her thinking time was interrupted when Sally Marriott came into the café, requesting to speak to her. When she noticed her red raw eyes and dishevelled appearance, Julia took Sally through to the kitchen.

"I suppose you've heard," Sally mumbled as she dabbed her nose with a shredded tissue. "Richard has called off the wedding."

No sooner had the words left Sally's lips did she double over, her mousy hair hanging over her eyes as she sobbed her heart out. Julia pulled the useless tissue from Sally's grip and replaced it with her own handkerchief from her dress pocket, which Sally gratefully accepted.

"I had heard, but I didn't want to assume it was true," Julia said softly, her hand rubbing the back of Sally's shoulders.

Sally paused her sobbing to smile at Julia, but

the smile quivered and the tears resumed almost instantly. She was a young woman in her mid-twenties and even through her upset, Julia could still see the natural English rose beauty radiating underneath. She had always admired Sally's looks from afar, and along with the rest of the village, had been surprised when she announced that she was marrying Richard May, who despite being handsome, was twenty years her senior.

"I thought I should tell you not to bother with the wedding cake," Sally said, sniffling into the handkerchief as the tears calmed down. "You can keep the deposit."

"I wouldn't dream of it," Julia said, already pulling her purse from her handbag, which was hanging from a hook on the wall. "Besides, I was having trouble making a cinnamon, rose and orange cake work."

Sally laughed softly, and Julia was glad to see a little lightness appear in her face before another flood of tears took over. She pushed the deposit she had taken into Sally's blouse pocket, sending a soft wink to the jilted girl. Julia knew what it felt like to have a man pull the rug from under her feet, and she knew how expensive starting out on your own could be.

"I should have seen it coming," Sally said, drying her eyes for the final time before inhaling deeply and looking up at the fluorescent lights in the kitchen's ceiling. "My mother always did say I wanted what I couldn't have."

Julia rubbed Sally's shoulder sympathetically, wondering if what she had heard about Sally '*carrying on*' with another man was true.

"Maybe there's a chance you'll reunite?"

"There isn't," Sally said, letting out a bitter laugh. "He's already cancelled the venue and told his parents it's over. He's so angry. I'm such a stupid girl. I tried to talk to him at Peridale Manor yesterday, but he refused to talk to me."

"You were at the garden party yesterday?" Julia asked. "I didn't see you."

"I only went to find Richard, but he wouldn't speak to me. I wanted to talk to him, to explain, but he pushed me away and he left. And then I heard about – *about* -,"

Sally didn't finish her sentence. Her sobbing started afresh, harder and heavier than ever before. Julia took Sally into her arms, and the crying woman clung to her like a baby to its mother. Through the beaded curtain, Julia could see Jessie and the few customers, her gran being one of them, all staring into the kitchen to see what was happening.

When Sally finally pulled away and handed back Julia's handkerchief, she shook out her mousy hair and composed herself.

"I've still got to see the florist and the dressmaker," Sally said, her bottom lip trembling, but no tears appearing. "All I ever wanted was the fairy tale wedding."

Julia knew she should tell her that she was still young and there was still time, but her own experience of the so-called fairy tale had jaded her. Instead, she wanted to tell Sally that it was overrated, and even if she walked down the aisle with Richard, *'till death do us part'* could really mean *'until I leave you for my young secretary'*. Julia decided neither were appropriate, so she offered Sally a drink and a cake on the house, both of which she declined. Julia let Sally leave out of the backdoor to avoid getting caught up in being questioned by the villagers.

"So?" Dot asked, looking at Julia expectantly along with the other villagers. "What did she say?"

"Whatever she said was said to me in confidence."

"Didn't you find out if the rumours about her and Charles Wellington having an affair were true?" Dot asked, her eyes wide and her mouth practically salivating.

"It wasn't my place to ask."

There was a loud groan from the watching crowd, and they quickly dispersed, some of them sitting, and some of them leaving as if they had only come for the gossip. Julia wondered if they had seen Sally entering the café and decided to follow her. How many people would suddenly find themselves in the florist and dressmakers?

After Dot told Julia and Jessie that they were having dinner at her house that afternoon because she had some lamb chops that needed to be eaten, Julia retreated back to the kitchen and pulled her notepad from her bag.

Flipping to a fresh page, she wrote Charles' name in the middle and circled it. She reluctantly drew an arrow from Charles and added her father's name. Less reluctantly, she drew another arrow and wrote Katie's name, followed by a line connecting the two. Next, she added two more arrows and two more names, which were also connected. She stared at Sally and Richard's names, adding a question mark next to the latters.

After witnessing the fight between Richard and Charles, the village had come to the conclusion that Charles was somehow involved in Richard calling off

Lemonade and Lies

his engagement to Sally. After seeing Sally and looking into her eyes, Julia felt like she had all but confirmed this to be true. She traced over the question mark next to Richard's name, wondering if a broken heart could drive a man to commit murder.

At the end of the workday, Julia and Jessie drove back to her cottage to pick up a pecan pie that was chilling in her fridge. Her gran didn't specifically ask Julia to bring dessert, but if she didn't they would be eating something that came out of a packet.

As the first signs of night started to tickle the pale sky, they pulled up outside of Julia's cottage. Julia killed the engine and unbuckled her seatbelt, while Jessie continued to stare blankly ahead, not seeming to notice they had even stopped.

"Is everything okay?" Julia asked softly, making Jessie jump. "You've been quiet today."

Julia didn't want to mention she had noticed Jessie growing increasingly quieter over the past week, although it hadn't gone unnoticed that it had started around the same time as the sleepwalking.

"I'm just tired," Jessie said with a shrug. "It's nothing."

"Am I working you too hard at the café?"

"It's nothing like that. Like I said, I'm just

tired."

Julia smiled softly at Jessie, who strained to smile back. Jessie was filled with so much passion and energy, so she hated seeing her young lodger's fire being dimmed. Julia had never wished to read another person's mind as much as she did in that moment.

They got out of the car and walked towards Julia's cottage. Further down the lane, her elderly neighbour, Emily Burns, was pruning her immaculate rose bushes. She spotted Julia and vigorously waved her over.

"Let yourself in," Julia whispered into Jessie's ear. "Emily is waving to me, and if I don't go and talk to her, I have a feeling she's going to hack my door down with those pruning shears."

Jessie accepted the keys, letting out a small laugh, and Julia was pleased to see her smiling again. She watched Jessie unlock the cottage door and walk into the darkness, stepping over a large stack of letters as she did.

"Good evening, Emily," Julia said as she approached Emily's low wall. "Your roses are looking exceptional."

"That's so kind of you to say, Julia," Emily said as she yanked off her gardening gloves. "You'll never guess what I heard earlier today."

Julia wondered if she should start to guess, but she decided saying nothing was the best option. No matter how she approached the topic, Emily would divulge everything she wanted to say.

"I heard something quite interesting walking back from my hair appointment this afternoon," Emily said, pushing up her greying curls for emphasis. "I don't usually pass Richard and Sally's cottage, but I fancied stretching my legs seeing as it was such a lovely day. Well, I say it was a lovely day, but it was ruined by the screaming and shouting that was coming from Richard and Sally's, or should I just say Richard's cottage, if the rumours of Sally's infidelity are to be believed."

Julia smiled and listened, not wanting to add that she knew those rumours were true.

"It was so loud, I practically heard every word. Your name came up more than once."

"My name? Are you sure?"

"It's a small village, Julia," Emily said, leaning over her freshly pruned rose bush, her eyes twinkling devilishly at being the one to break the information. "Unless there is another Julia who bakes cakes, I'm more than sure it was you."

"What were they saying?"

"Oh, nothing much," Emily said, waving her hand. "That wasn't the interesting part. Sally was crying about how she had visited your café to cancel her wedding cake order, but she was telling Richard how it wasn't too late and that you were an understanding woman. The poor girl was begging for his forgiveness, mind you, I never thought they were suitable. My own husband was older than me, but those two always seemed odd. If you ask me, I'd say Sally was after Richard's money. You know he inherited a fortune from his father? Richard Senior was a lance corporal in the army, and he was a thrifty saver. The money had barely hit Richard's account when Sally started sniffing around."

"What did you hear that was so interesting?" Julia asked, wanting to get to the point.

Emily could barely contain her smile. She looked up and down the lane to make sure it was clear, before leaning so far into the rose bush that the thorns snagged and tugged at her blouse.

"Sally told Richard that she loved him, and nobody else," Emily whispered. "Richard replied by saying, and I quote, *'you think because he's dead, I'm going to forgive you?'*"

Emily leaned back and pulled the thorns out of her blouse. She brushed down the stray strands and folded her hands over her chest, far too pleased with herself to care about the state of her garment. When Julia didn't respond, Emily's smile turned to a frown, and she leaned in again.

"You know what that means, don't you?" Emily whispered again, her eyes darting up and down the lane. "Sally was having an affair with Charles Wellington, and Richard found out, that's why they were fighting at your step-mother's garden party."

"She's not my step-mother," Julia found herself saying. "It's been lovely chatting Emily, but my gran is expecting me for dinner. Have a lovely evening."

Before Emily could engage Julia in more gossiping, Julia turned on her heels and walked as quickly as her legs would take her back to her cottage. If she hadn't just discovered that Sally had been at the garden party, the news of the affair wouldn't have bothered Julia so much, but her mind was spinning so quickly, she didn't immediately notice that the stack of letters on her doormat was thinner than when Jessie had opened the door. Julia crept down the hallway, and peered into Jessie's open bedroom door, just as Jessie was folding a letter and cramming it back into an envelope. She opened her wardrobe, curled the letter up, and crammed it down into one of her boots.

Julia stepped back, not wanting Jessie to know what she had just seen. Julia didn't know what was contained within that letter, but she was more than sure it was linked to Jessie's sudden shift in mood.

"Ready?" Julia asked, stepping forward again when she heard Jessie close the wardrobe door.

"Do you mind if I stay here and get an early night?" Jessie asked, forcing forward what appeared to be a fake yawn. "Dot won't mind."

Julia almost protested, but stopped herself. She thrust forward her kindest smile and nodded, telling Jessie where the rarely used takeaway menus were if she got hungry later. Reluctantly leaving her alone in the cottage, no doubt leaving her to pour over the contents of the mysterious letter, Julia fed Mowgli, grabbed her pecan pie, and drove back into the village.

CHAPTER 7

J ulia could barely get a knife through Dot's lamb chops, but she battled through, smirking across the table to Sue every time one of their knives slipped from the tough meat.

"That was delicious," Sue said after finishing and pushing her plate away, sending a wink to Julia. "Your homemade mint sauce really complimented the lamb."

"Homemade?" Dot scoffed as she cut her last piece of lamb in half, her tiny arms working double speed. "You know I don't have time for that nonsense. Me and some of the girls had our second weekly book club meeting just before you girls got here. I barely had time to throw the chops into the frying pan."

Julia wanted to ask how she had managed to cook them twice through if she hadn't had time, but she held her tongue.

"Book club?" Julia asked. "Is that new?"

"Well, our poker club was rumbled by your boyfriend," Dot said, rolling her eyes as she started to gather the plates. "I simply asked him the laws regarding gambling in the privacy of one's home, and he took quite the exception to it. Started asking all of these questions, so I told the girls it was better if we switched things up for a while until he stopped sniffing around."

"What book are you reading?" Sue asked.

"Fifty Shades of Grey," Dot said casually. "It was the only book in the charity shop with enough copies for all of us."

Sue and Julia both bit their lips at the same time to stop their laughter from bursting out. Whenever Julia thought she had her gran figured out, she would say something that would prove her wrong.

After the plates were cleared away, Dot brought Julia's pecan pie from the fridge, along with a small bowl of clotted cream. She served up three generous slices, leaving one for Julia to take home to Jessie.

"Delicious as always Julia," Dot mumbled through a large mouthful. "I'm not usually a fan of that American food, but I have to say that this is quite lovely."

"Just something I'm thinking of putting on the menu," Julia said. "Read about it in a cookbook Jessie got from the library and it intrigued me."

"Jessie can read?" Dot asked, a brow darting up. "I thought she was raised on the streets?"

"*Gran!*" Sue cried.

"What?"

"Don't be so mean!" Sue said, shaking her head at Julia. "Jessie is a lovely girl."

"Did I say otherwise?" Dot snapped. "I'm just stating facts. The girl was raised on the streets, wasn't she Julia?"

"She was living on the streets for about six months, Gran. Before that, she was living with foster parents."

"Poor girl," Dot said. "It's not like she's had the best life. I doubt her education has been consistent throughout her life. How is she? I'm surprised not to see her with you tonight."

Julia crammed her mouth full of pecan pie, wondering if she should reveal her worries to her family. She decided if she told them, they might be able to give her advice on what she should do.

"She told me she was tired, but she's hiding something from me," Julia said after licking clotted cream from her lips. "She's been sleepwalking too."

"You used to sleepwalk," Dot said. "Scared the wits out of me at first."

Julia stared ahead at Sue, not realising that her gran was talking to her.

"I used to sleepwalk?" Julia asked, her brows pinching together as she dropped her fork, suddenly no longer hungry. "I don't remember that."

"Well, you wouldn't. I never told you. It was right after your poor mother died. You used to get up in the dead of the night to sit by the window, staring out. I thought you were a burglar at first. You almost got a ceramic cat bashed over your head the first time I caught you."

Julia stared down at her pecan pie, wondering why she had no memory of this. She looked at Sue, who shrugged. It was possible her gran was just confused, but Julia doubted she would make up such a thing.

"How long did it last?" Julia asked, her voice low, almost ashamed.

"You grew out of it eventually," Dot said, tapping her finger on her chin as she thought. "In fact, I could have sworn it only happened in the times when your father was away. Yes, that's right. I remember telling him that you were getting up and looking for his car to pull up outside. I think you eventually realised his trips home were getting less frequent and it seeped through to your subconscious."

Julia tried to conjure some memory of it happening, but nothing came forth. She thought of her twelve-year-old self sitting by her gran's sitting room window in the dark, staring out at the village green waiting for something that would never come. Her chest tightened.

"I find it best to just confront things head on," Sue said carefully, seeming to recognise the hurt in Julia's expression. "Just ask her what's on her mind. Even if you don't think she wants to talk about it, she might just need a little coaxing."

Julia couldn't touch her pecan pie after that, so when Sue and her gran finished, she cleared the plates away herself, and took her time washing them in the small kitchen sink. When she was finished, she joined them in the sitting room for tea. Julia sat in the armchair furthest from the window, finding it difficult to look in its direction.

"Has your boyfriend said anything about this murder case?" Dot asked after blowing and sipping tea from her small china cup.

"Barker isn't my boyfriend," Julia said, hearing the bite in her voice. "I haven't seen him since the garden party."

"I'm surprised how little information is floating around the village," Dot said, scrunching up her face and staring hopefully at the small red telephone in the corner. "You would think somebody would know something? Did you know Joanne Lewis' husband was working on Katie's silly spa idea?"

"Where did you hear that?" Sue asked, clearly not having heard that information herself.

"I saw Terry at the garden party," Dot said, her eyes suddenly narrowing as if she had just landed on some information she had forgotten she possessed. "Well, I saw him on my way back from the bathroom. It was right before I came out and saw you all huddled around the body."

"You saw Terry in Peridale Manor?" Julia asked, her ears pricking up. "Upstairs?"

"I used the downstairs bathroom," Dot said, shaking her head. "You don't suppose I was in the house at the same time that poor man was pushed from the window, do you?"

"It's possible," Julia said, sipping her tea and leaning forward. "What did Terry say to you?"

"I was just asking what he was doing in the house," Dot said, tapping her chin once more. "Yes, that's right. He was wearing work boots and he stood out like a sore thumb in that house. He had just come in from the garden for some water. He told me he had gotten the contract for the work, and that he was digging out the pool. I told him how ridiculous the spa idea was, and then I came outside, and well, we all know what happened next."

"Which direction was he heading in?" Julia asked.

"Direction?" Dot asked with a frown. "Why does it matter? The kitchen, I think."

"Not the staircase?"

Dot thought about it for a moment, looking from Sue and Julia, her mouth opening and closing. She seemed frustrated by all of the questions.

"It might have been," Dot said, tugging at the brooch fastened to her collar under her chin. "I'm an old woman. My memory isn't what it was, girls. The staircase and the kitchen are in the same direction, so maybe."

"I visited Peridale Manor yesterday," Julia said quietly as she stared ahead, her mind working overtime. "Katie told me that Dad was being questioned by the police, and that he had been at the station all day. Then I saw Joanne Lewis, and she told me about Terry getting the contract."

"Your father was being questioned?" Dot asked, her frown deepening. "Why?"

"I don't know yet," Julia said dismissively. "What I do know is that Joanne specifically told me her and Terry were both outside at the time of Charles' death."

"Oh," Dot said, her hand drifting up to her mouth. "*Oh!* Have I just uncovered something?"

"Perhaps," Julia said, not wanting to get her gran excited. "He could have quickly gone back outside again. Wrong place, wrong time."

Sue sighed and pinched between her brows. Julia could sense what was coming next.

"Julia," Sue started, looking her sister deep in the eyes. "Why do I feel like you're investigating this?"

"Because I am," Julia said, already reaching for her pad to scribble down what Dot had just revealed.

"I think the police are trying to pin this murder on Katie or Dad."

"Do you think either of them did it?" Dot asked, her voice suddenly small.

"I don't know," Julia said. "Either way, I want to know, and if they are arrested, I want to be absolutely sure there is no room for error."

Dot's eyes widened excitedly, but Sue sighed again and shook her head. Julia knew her sister was just worried about her. She didn't understand Julia's need to find out all of the facts. Julia didn't understand it much herself, it was just a drive she had within her. It was a similar feeling she had whenever she tasted one of her cakes and she was trying to put her finger on why it didn't quite taste right.

"I'll keep an ear to the ground," Dot exclaimed, snapping her fingers together as she ran towards the phone. "In fact, I'll start calling around to see if people have heard anything."

Julia wasn't interested in idle village gossip, she was interested in finding out the truth about what had led to somebody pushing a man out of a window at a garden party. Somebody had murdered Charles Wellington, and her list of suspects was growing by the day. She added 'Terry Lewis' alongside Katie and her father, and Sally and Richard. Flipping back a page, she added *'find out if Terry had a connection to Charles'*.

Dropping her notepad back into her bag, she quickly finished her tea and made her excuses to go home so she could shut herself in her bedroom with her notes and her thoughts.

CHAPTER 8

On Julia's drive back up to her cottage, she was so distracted that she almost didn't notice Barker getting out of his car. She slowed down, pulling up behind him. When he spotted her, a smile spread across his face, which had the ability to make Julia forget what had been swirling around in her mind.

"Evening," Barker said, leaning his hand heavily

against the top of her car as she rolled down her window. "Bit late to only just be closing the café, isn't it?"

"Dinner at Gran's," Julia said. "I could say the same about you. I suspect the investigation is keeping you all busy."

Barker pursed his lips, and he almost seemed disappointed in Julia for heading straight to the investigation. She tightened her fingers around the steering wheel, inhaling deeply, trying to rid her mind of it for a moment.

"Can I invite you in for some tea?" Barker asked, glancing awkwardly back to his cottage. "Or some coffee?"

Julia heard the nerves in Barker's voice, and they mirrored the ones that had suddenly sprung up in her stomach. She peered past Barker's car into the dark, imagining her cottage in the distance.

"Do you have peppermint and liquorice tea?" Julia asked.

"They make that?" Barker asked, a brow darting up. "I have black tea."

"Good job I carry my own," Julia said as she reached into her handbag to pull out an individually wrapped teabag.

Julia jumped out of her car and followed Barker

through the dark, and into his cottage. It was small and similar in layout to Julia's, but everything else was completely different. Where Julia's cottage was neat and tidy with appropriate furniture for a period building, Barker's home was messy, filled with stacks of boxes he still hadn't unpacked, and glossy furniture that would have better suited an apartment in the city.

"I've been meaning to unpack those," Barker said when he caught Julia staring at the brown boxes. "It's been a bit busier than I expected."

They walked through to his small sitting room, which was equally as messy. Pizza boxes and coffee cups cluttered the table, along with paperwork and golfing magazines. Barker turned on a couple of lamps, gathered up the papers, and cleared the shiny leather couch for Julia.

"I had a cleaner at my last place," Barker said, his cheeks blushing. "I've been meaning to find one in Peridale. Either that, or I adjust to cleaning up my own mess."

"You're a busy man," Julia said, not wanting to shame him for the mess. "There is a cleaning agency in the village. I'll see if I can get their number for you."

"That would be great," Barker said as he

accepted Julia's wrapped teabag. "Make yourself comfy. I'll get the kettle on."

Barker hurried off to the kitchen, ducking so he didn't hit his head on the beams. Julia couldn't decide if the cottage didn't suit Barker, or if Barker didn't suit the cottage. He had been living in the village for over a month now. It already felt like he had been there as long as everybody else, but looking at his glossy furniture and packed boxes reminded Julia how different he really was.

"Smells delicious," Barker said, sniffing Julia's tea as he walked back in clutching two mismatching mugs. "I've always been a coffee man myself."

"Two sugars?"

"You remembered," Barker said with a nod. "Impressive."

"It's a talent," Julia said, accepting her mug. "Or a curse. Depending on how you look at it. There's not a villager's order in the café that I seem to be able to forget, even if I wanted to."

Barker sat in an armchair across from Julia and stared ahead at the blank TV, which Julia noticed hadn't even been plugged in. She remembered moving into her own cottage, eager to unpack everything to feel right at home as quickly as possible. Adjusting from the city to Peridale had taken her minutes, not months, but she had been born there. She wondered what it must feel like to come to such a small village and be thrown into its hustle and bustle with no time to acclimatise.

"I heard you were interviewing my father," Julia said, trying and failing to drop it casually into the silence.

Barker smirked as he sipped his steaming hot coffee. He reached out and placed the coffee mug on top of a golfing magazine before leaning back in his chair to rest his fingers over his creased white shirt and tie.

"I don't like to rule anybody out," Barker said. "For what it's worth, I don't think he did it."

"Did his feet not match the footprints you found?" Julia asked, again trying and failing to sound casual.

"How do you know about those?"

"I noticed them when I was at the manor."

Barker narrowed his eyes on Julia, a smirk tickling his lips. He sighed and rubbed his eyes heavily with his hands before sitting straight up and leaning against the chair's arm. The armchair didn't look particularly comfortable, but neither was the couch under her.

"You don't miss a trick, do you, Julia?"

"I try not to."

"No, his feet didn't match those boot prints, not that we've found the boots yet," Barker said. "It doesn't mean he's innocent. Those boot prints could have been made at any time before the murder."

"Actually, between about midday and the murder," Julia corrected him. "When I went to the bathroom earlier in the day, the boot prints weren't there."

"And you only just think to mention this now?" Barker asked, his nostrils flaring.

"You told me to stay out of things," Julia said quietly before taking another sip of her tea. "I'm just doing what you told me."

Barker stared at her, and for a moment he appeared angry, but his scowl turned into a warm smile. He let out a small laugh and shook his head. Leaning his arm on the chair and resting his head on his knuckles, he stared at Julia.

"Did you manage to figure out what was missing from the plinth next to the window?" Julia asked.

"Katie couldn't remember what was there," Barker said. "Neither could your father. Vincent Wellington barely knows what day it is. I don't even think he realises his son has died."

"It's a sad situation," Julia said. "It's no life to

have."

"I can't help but feel your step-mother is taking advantage of his state."

"She's not my step-mother," Julia quickly added. "She just happens to be married to my father. We're the same age, you know?"

"She looks much older," Barker said with a small wink. "Did you know she used to be a glamour model? When I was investigating the house, I was surprised to see very explicit pictures of her hung all over her bedroom."

"Sounds like Katie," Julia said. "Self-indulgent and superficial to the core. She told me she was only doing this spa thing because she was bored."

Julia recognised the venom in her voice, forcing her to sit up and sip her tea. She thought back to what her gran had told her about her sleepwalking, and the lingering resentment towards her father bubbled stronger than it had in over two decades. That resentment had found a new target in Katie, and she hated herself for being that way.

"One of my officers saw you snooping around Peridale Manor yesterday," Barker said, seeming to sense Julia's thoughts.

"And what makes you so sure that was me?"

"I gave them your exact description and told

them to watch out for you," Barker said. "Even I didn't expect you to jump so quickly into this one."

"I was visiting my family."

"The family you're not even that close to?" Barker asked, leaning forward a little. "I asked your father about his relationships. He filled me in a little."

"You were asking my father about me?" Julia asked quietly, her brow reflectively arching.

"It was just routine. We ask all sorts of questions to establish a profile of somebody. He didn't say much, just that you two weren't close."

Julia sipped her tea, wondering if that was true, or if Barker had purposefully asked her father questions about her to try and figure her out. As the sweet liquorice coated her throat, she wasn't sure if she should be offended or flattered.

"My father's feet are quite big, aren't they?" Julia asked suddenly.

"Yes? Why?"

"Size twelve?" Julia asked. "Maybe eleven?"

"Eleven," Barker said, his eyes narrowing. "Why do you ask?"

"Because I'm just trying to establish the size of the boot prints found at the scene. If they didn't fit my father, I'm guessing they were smaller, rather than larger? I'd say size thirteen, even for a man, is a little on the large size. I'd also say it wasn't a ten either. It's possible to fit your foot into a boot one size smaller, even if it will be a little uncomfortable. The way you said my father's foot didn't fit makes me think it didn't fit by a long way because you sounded rather disappointed that your obvious suspect didn't quite fit into the frame, which was why you suggested the boot prints may be unrelated, even though we both know they were. So, my guess is that the prints found at the scene were either a seven, or an eight? From my memory, they didn't look much smaller than that, which means the murderer has either size seven, or eight feet, or maybe even a little smaller, but not too much smaller. Just like you can fit your feet into a size smaller, you could fit your feet into boots a little bigger, but not too much bigger because boots that large would be too heavy to produce such clear footprints if the boots drastically didn't fit a person. Am I thinking along the right lines here, Detective?"

Julia paused to sip her tea and enjoy the look of complete shock that had slowly spread across Barker's face. She had stitched together the theory in the back of her mind over the last couple of minutes, but it made complete sense to her.

"If this was a couple hundred years ago, you would have been burned at the stake for being a witch," Barker said, his eyes widening. "You know that, right?"

"I'll take that as a compliment, and also that I was right."

"I didn't say that."

"But you didn't correct me," Julia said, her hands closing around the warm mug. "If I had been wildly wrong, you would have tried to correct me, Detective Inspector. I know you're not a man who puts a lot of stock into his pride, but you are a man, which means you like to be right."

"What makes you think I don't put stock into my pride?" Barker asked, his eyes widening as though he really were sitting in the company of a witch.

"Because if you were a proud man, you wouldn't have invited a woman into your cottage when it looks like this," Julia said as she rested her half finished tea on the cluttered coffee table. "Thank you for the boiled water."

"You're leaving already?" Barker jumped up, his head almost hitting the low ceiling.

"Jessie will be wondering where I am. Unless you want to sit around for the rest of the night discussing the finer details of your case?"

Barker let out a small laugh of disbelief, and Julia revelled in the fact that she had clearly trumped him more than once. When she had first met Barker, she knew he underestimated her, and even though she knew he no longer did, she still enjoyed being one step ahead of him. Just like when she was following somebody else's recipe for a cake she had never baked before, she liked to guess the next step before reading it. More often than not, her logical thinking proved her right.

"You're an extraordinary woman, Julia Smith," Barker said as he led her towards the front door. "I can easily say I have never met a woman quite like you."

"Should I take that as a compliment?" she asked as she fished her car keys from her pocket.

"I'm not quite sure," Barker said as he leaned around her to open the front door. "What I am sure of is that I'm going to ask you out on a date, and this time I won't take no for an answer."

Julia stepped out of his cottage, dropping her curls over her face to conceal her sudden blushing.

"I wasn't intending to say no."

"I'll pick you up tomorrow at seven," Barker said.

"I look forward to it," Julia replied, the butterflies in her stomach swirling around so hard that they were crashing into one another. "One more thing, Detective Inspector. Size seven, or size eight?"

"I'm sorry?"

"The boots. Seven or eight?" Julia said, her fingers gripping around her keys. "For my own piece of mind."

"That would be telling, wouldn't it?" Barker said, his usual smug smirk returning at being able to trump Julia back. "Goodnight, Julia."

Julia walked casually back to her car, and set off up the lane. Just before Barker's cottage faded from view, she glanced back in her rear-view mirror to see Barker still standing on his doorstep, looking towards her car. The man she had only known for a month was making her feel excited in a way that her husband of sixteen years had failed to.

Back in her cottage, she was disappointed to see Jessie asleep on top of her bed, not because her lodger had fallen asleep, but because she appeared to be pretending to have done so. It only confirmed to Julia that there was something she didn't want to talk about.

Julia made a mental note to investigate two things; she wanted to revisit Peridale Manor to speak to her father, and she wanted to check Jessie's wardrobe to see what she was hiding.

CHAPTER 9

Julia left Jessie in charge of the café the next morning for the first time so she could visit Peridale Manor alone. Dark clouds circled above the house as she drove towards it, blocking out the blue sky Julia had awoken to. In Julia's mind, the dark clouds had been circling all morning. She couldn't shake the feeling she was being lied to by more than one person.

Lemonade and Lies

"Julia," her dad exclaimed after Hilary let her into the house, putting up less of a fight this time. "I wasn't expecting to see you today. Can I get you a cup of tea, or coffee?"

"Tea would be lovely," Julia said as she reached into her handbag to grab a teabag. "I've brought my own."

"Peppermint and liquorice?" he mumbled as he read over the label. "How – *unusual*. I'm sure it tastes more delicious than it sounds."

Julia's father handed the teabag to Hilary, who eyed it disdainfully. Brian stepped to the side and let Julia lead the way through the house to the grand sitting room.

"This is one of the rooms we're turning into a treatment room," he said as he sat on an uncomfortable looking antique sofa. "It has beautiful views of the grounds, although I dare say it's going to rain today."

Julia looked out of the floor-to-ceiling windows where she could see a team of four working on the new pool. It appeared they were getting ready to pour concrete into the foundations they had dug.

"Is Katie home today?" Julia asked after Hilary brought through their tea on a heavy silver tray.

"She's gone to London for the day for a

shopping trip with some of the girls, to take her mind off things. You know what it's like."

Julia didn't know what it was like. She didn't have a brother, but if she did, she couldn't imagine a shopping trip taking her mind off his murder. She tried to imagine the pain she would feel if Sue were taken from her so cruelly, but it was impossible to summon.

"She seems to be coping quite well," Julia said as she sipped her hot tea. "Were they close?"

"Not as close as she would have liked. He was rather jealous of her."

"Jealous?" Julia asked, remembering the argument she had overheard between them. "Because she is Vincent's favourite?"

Brian's lips quivered, appearing confused by Julia's knowledge of their relationship. She busied herself by blowing on her hot tea, wishing she had kept that information closer to her chest.

"Parents don't have favourites," he said with a small shrug. "We just love our children differently."

Julia attempted to ignore the irony in what he had just said. If Vincent cared differently for each of his children, Brian cared equally indifferently for his own.

"This isn't my first time here to talk to you,"

Julia said, resting her tea on the edge of the awkwardly shaped antique sofa. "I was here two days ago, but you were busy."

"Katie mentioned your visit," he said, giving a non-convincing smile. "I suppose she told you where I was? The police were simply just trying to eliminate me because I live here."

"And did they eliminate you?"

"Of course they did," he said with a small laugh, the suspicion on his face growing. "You don't think I could push a man from a window, do you?"

Julia didn't know what to think. She didn't like the thought of her father committing a murder, but she didn't know the man sitting in front of her as much as he was pretending. She remembered what Barker had told her about the boots not fitting, so she shook her head and reached for her tea.

"And Katie?" Julia asked, wanting to steer the conversation towards the purpose of her visit. "Have they eliminated her yet?"

"It's not as simple as that," he said, leaning forward to rest his elbows on his knees. "Why do I feel like I'm being interrogated by my own daughter?"

"I'm just curious. I was here. Everybody was here. We all just want to figure this out as much as I suppose you do."

"There's no *supposing* about it," he said, his voice growing a little darker. "Charles and I never particularly saw eye to eye. There was a reason it appeared Vincent favoured his daughter. Charles was a loose cannon, a troublemaker some might say. Vincent's money is old family money, but there's less of it left than people assume. If Charles had had his way, he would have gambled away every penny the moment he inherited his share of Peridale Manor and it's dwindling fortune. When Katie suggested to her father that they turn this place into a spa, he was happy to consent. Of course, this was before his last stroke. He doesn't talk much these days. In fact, he doesn't do much at all. If he knows his son is dead, he's not grieving. Charles wasn't a nice man, nor was he kind to his sister or father. He lived recklessly, surfing from couch to couch. He burned through his trust fund in a matter of years and had been living off hand-outs from his father. Katie is an entrepreneur. She is invested in giving this old place a purpose. She has vision, unlike her brother. She saw the Wellington name becoming a brand so future generations would reap what she had sown. All her brother cared about was getting his cut and wasting it."

"Future generations?" Julia choked, her minty tea catching the back of her throat. "I didn't think Katie or Charles had kids."

Brian squirmed uncomfortably in his seat, telling Julia everything she needed to know. She remembered how scared she had been of the announcement, and how relieved she had been when her fears had been proven wrong.

"I wasn't going to tell you girls until it was official," Brian said with a heavy sigh. "We're trying for a baby, but it's not easy. We're having – *complications*."

"A baby?" Julia mumbled, her cheeks burning red. "Don't you think you're -,"

"Too old?"

"Maybe just a little."

Brian exhaled heavily, leaning back in his chair. He stared ahead at Julia with sadness in his eyes, and for a brief moment, Julia thought she saw years of regret flash through them. In that split second, Julia was looking at the father she was still clinging to in the back of her mind.

"We have a lot to offer a child," Brian said in a rehearsed way. "The Wellington name must continue somehow."

"You're not a Wellington," Julia found herself

saying without thinking about it. "You're a South."

"Well, the baby would be a Wellington-South. You get the idea."

"I do," Julia said, her jaw gritting tightly. "Very clearly."

At that moment, as if on cue, the heavens opened. Heavy rain pounded down on Peridale Manor, scattering the workman like ants. Julia and her father sipped their tea in silence as they listened to the pitter-patter of rain echo throughout the old manor.

"Was there anything else, Julia?" her father asked as he stood up. "I have a meeting at noon with some old antiques contacts to ask about furniture for the spa."

Julia finished her tea, and placed it back on the silver tray. She followed him in standing, knowing she had dozens of unanswered questions, but she was unable to think of anything other than a tiny screaming baby who would be her brother or sister.

"There was one thing," Julia said, gathering her thoughts, trying to think of what was the most important. "After Charles was pushed, I noticed something had been taken from one of the display plinths next the window. Do you know what was there?"

"Ah, yes. The detective asked me that too," he said with a small nod, his finger napping his chin. "I'm afraid I don't. Katie doesn't either. This house is so big and full of so much junk, neither of us can recall what was there. Vincent would probably know, but it's almost impossible to get a word out of the poor man. Is it important?"

"I'm sure it's not," Julia lied, not wanting to let him know that she thought the missing item was a possible murder weapon. "Can I use your bathroom before I go?"

"Of course," he said as they walked back through to the grand entrance hall. "It's upstairs, second door on the left."

Julia hurried up the staircase, feeling her father's eyes on her with every step. She turned the corner, and walked towards the bathroom, making her way further down to hall. The broken window had already been replaced, making it feel like nothing had happened at all. The display plinth was still empty, but the dust had since been polished away. Julia knew there was one overlooked person in the house who would know exactly what had been there, but she was sure that Hilary wouldn't be so quick to offer Julia any information.

After a minute passed, Julia turned to walk back

towards the staircase. If her father had been there, she would have had to make her way back downstairs and abandon her plan. Luckily, he wasn't, so she hurried along the hallway, her tiny kitten heels clicking loudly on the polished mahogany floorboards.

The layout of the manor was a mystery to her, with dozens of different doors lining the long hall. Very soon, those rooms would be full of spa visitors enjoying whatever Katie had to offer them.

Along with the murder, the spa was also a popular topic of conversation in her café at the moment, with most of the villagers firmly against it, even if they were offering free use of the pool to residents during the week. As a business owner, Julia was undecided. The new tourists in town would likely give her profits a little boost, but the thought of the village changing in any way made her tummy ache. While the rest of the world was constantly shifting and evolving, Peridale had stayed as it always had, and that's why she loved it.

Ignoring all of the other doors, Julia went straight to the room Katie and Charles had been arguing in, on the morning of his death. On her way, she caught a glimpse of Vincent sitting in front of a TV in his wheelchair. She thought they locked eyes, but she decided it was her imagination playing tricks on her.

After knocking softly on the wood, Julia crept into the room when there was no reply. She realised instantly that this was her father and Katie's room. The nude portraits of Katie that Barker had spoken of littered the walls. Julia wasn't a prude, but the narcissism made her feel uneasy. The wallpaper behind the portraits was blood red and ink black damask, giving the room a seedier feeling than the rest of the manor.

Ignoring all of this, Julia went straight to the walk-in closet to find exactly what she was looking for. The floor was lined with hundreds of pairs of designer heels. Julia didn't understand what a woman could do with so many pairs of shoes. She owned a couple of pairs of work shoes, some flat and some with small heels depending on how she felt, and a single pair of black high heels, which she had only worn once, despite Sue buying them for her years ago.

Julia plucked a shoe out at random to look at the size printed on the sole. Just to be sure, she picked up a couple more shoes to check they were all the same size, which they were. They were all size eight, which was an above average size for a woman

Katie's height, but not uncommon.

Leaving the shoes exactly where she had found them, Julia turned and walked back into the bedroom knowing her father could walk in at any moment. On her way past the window she looked out into the rain. The heavy clouds circled above, making it look as though it was virtually dusk, not nearly noon.

She then noticed a yellow light in the darkness. Squinting, she spotted the builder's cabin stationed at the far end of the garden. Next to the cabin, the rain was bouncing off the roof of a car she immediately recognised as Joanne's. The Lewis house had been next on Julia's list, so she hurried out of the bedroom and down the stairs, ready to kill two birds with one stone.

"Ah, there you are," her father said, appearing from a door when she reached the bottom of the stairs. "I thought you had already gone."

"Women's troubles," she said quickly, knowing he wouldn't ask any more questions. "Dad, can I ask you something?"

"Of course you can," he said, suddenly looking nervous.

"Where were you when Charles was pushed from the window?"

Lemonade and Lies

Brian pursed his lips and folded his arms across his chest, appearing to be considering if he should tell Julia. She knew she was going out on a limb, but he had told her the truth about him and Katie trying for a baby, so it was worth a shot.

"I was in the grounds looking for Katie," he said, his eyes dark and piercing. "After Charles ruined her speech, she ran off looking for him. When she didn't find him in the house, she ran off into the grounds before I could stop her. I went looking for her, but I couldn't find her, so I went back to the house where she was drinking whiskey in my study. She said she couldn't find him so she looped around and came to find me, but needed something to calm her nerves. Then we came out, and that's when we saw what had happened."

"Is that what you told the police?" Julia asked.

"I told them the truth," he said with a firm nod. "I know what you're trying to suggest, Julia. Katie didn't kill her brother."

"I should get going," Julia said, setting off towards the door. "I've left Jessie in charge of the café."

Brian walked her to the grand entrance, opening the door for her. They stood and looked out into the rain for a moment. He looked as if he might say something, but he didn't. Julia wondered if he knew he had just told her that Katie's alibi was a lie, therefore putting her alone in the house at the time of her brother's murder. Were those boot prints really the boots Katie had put on in front of a crowd of people? Even if they were the right size, Julia didn't want to rule anything out yet, even if the evidence was mounting up.

Julia hurried through the rain towards her car, the shower instantly soaking her through. She flicked on her headlights, watching as the rain bounced against the gravel driveway. Her father lingered at the front door, so she started to reverse slowly into a U-turn. When he finally closed the door, she looped around and pulled up next to Joanne's car.

CHAPTER 10

J ulia jumped out of her car and walked past
Joanne's, the rain continuing to stick her dress
to her skin. Through the yellow light piercing
the closed blinds, there were two figures, one of
them pacing back and forth. Julia crept up the
couple of steps towards the door of the cabin. She
was about to knock, but through the din of the rain,
a woman's voice floated through. Pressing her ear up

against the white plastic door, she recognised the voice as Joanne's.

"You should be glad he's dead!" Joanne cried. "He's done us all a favour. Without this job, we'd be ruined."

"Joanne, just -," said a man, who she recognised as Terry.

"Don't tell me to calm down! You gambled away our future. You gambled away your son's future. We're hanging on by a thread, and this job is the only thing that is coming to save us. When was the last time you got us a job like this? *Huh*? You haven't in *years*. You got us into this mess, so you can fix it."

"Joanne, just listen -,"

"*Terry*!" she shrieked. "There's nothing you can say to make this better. I'm tired of this. I'm going, and if you know what's good for you, you won't follow me."

Julia quickly ducked under the window and darted around the far side of the building, pushing her body up against the cabin wall. She heard the door open and seconds later, Joanne's engine roared to life. Holding her breath and closing her eyes, she stood frozen against the wall as the rain pelted against her. She didn't dare breathe until Joanne's car drove past her and sped away from the cabin.

Lemonade and Lies

Not wanting to chance being caught by Terry, she walked around the back of the cabin, her tiny heels sinking into the mud. The suction of the mud pulled off her left shoe, her bare foot planting in the sludge, her toes dancing in the filth. Hands outstretched and water in her eyes she bent down to pick up her shoe, but she fell forward, landing hands and knees in the mud. It took all her power not to cry out.

She touched the heel of her shoe, so she pulled it out of the mud, deciding it was better to carry it back to her car. Soaked and filthy, she tiptoed through the torrent.

Keeping her headlights turned off, Julia reversed through the dark and drove quicker than she ever had, until she was pulling up outside of her cottage.

As she quickly showered so she could go back to the café clean and fresh, Joanne's words were circling around her mind.

'You should be glad he's dead. You got us into this mess.'

Julia hurried into her café under the protection of an umbrella. She wasn't surprised to see that it was almost empty, except for one customer. What she was surprised to see was Sally sitting at the table nearest the counter. When Jessie and Sally both turned to look at who had just walked through the door, they both looked extremely relieved to see Julia.

"I was beginning to think you would never come back," Jessie whispered to her as Julia hung her raincoat up in the kitchen. "There was a huge rush of people when the rain started."

"It's good practice," Julia said. "How long has Sally been here?"

"About twenty minutes," Jessie said as she looked down at Julia's dress. "You weren't wearing that when you left."

"It's a long story. I'll tell you later."

Julia adjusted her hair in the reflection of a knife, brushed down the creases in the blue dress she hadn't had time to iron, and walked through to the café and straight to Sally.

Julia noticed how different she looked from the last time she had seen her. It looked as though she had had a good night's sleep, her mousy hair was perfectly straight despite the rain, she was wearing a full face of makeup, and she was smiling. Julia sensed some nerves coming from Sally, but she understood them because she could guess what Sally was about to tell her.

"The wedding is back on," Sally said cautiously. "We've decided to give things another go."

"That's great news," Julia said, unsure if it was. "I suppose you're here to reorder your wedding cake?"

"You're a mind reader, Julia," Sally said, her fingers fumbling with her engagement ring. "Although can we just have a simple sponge this time? Richard never liked the idea of a cinnamon, rose and orange cake anyway."

Julia nodded, wondering if this second attempt at their engagement had come with some strict conditions. Looking into Sally's eyes, Julia sensed uneasiness in them, even if she was trying to hide it behind a smile. Her mascara and elaborate eye shadow were distracting, but not enough to hide the fact she had recently been crying.

"Forgive me if I'm talking out of turn, but I wanted to ask you a question about Charles," Julia said quietly, leaning across the table.

"Charles?" Sally's false smile suddenly dropped, and her bottom lip started to tremble. "What about him?"

Before Julia could say another word, her café door opened, and a dark figure walked in from the rain. They all turned to watch as Richard pulled his hood down, his eyes honing in on Sally.

"I've been waiting for you in the car," Richard said, his voice flat and empty.

"I was waiting for Julia to get back," Sally explained, the shake in her voice obvious.

"Have you asked her about the cake?"

"Yes."

"And told her you don't want that stupid flavour?"

"Yes."

"Then let's go," Richard said, his dark eyes landing on Julia as he reopened the door.

Sally pulled on her jacket, and without another word headed straight for Richard. Something red caught Julia's attention against the whiteness of her door. Richard's knuckles were covered in cuts, but they weren't fresh; they had started to scab over.

"What a weirdo," Jessie said loudly when they both left the café. "What does she see in him?"

"Sally dreams of the happily ever after. She will do whatever it takes to get it, even if that means sacrifice."

"I think women like that are dumb," Jessie said, smacking her gum against her tongue, which Julia had told her she wasn't allowed to chew behind the counter. "You wouldn't catch me dead bowing to a man like that."

"I did for a while," Julia said, holding her hand out under Jessie's mouth for her to spit out the gum. "When Richard attacked Charles at the garden party, did he actually hit him?"

Jessie reluctantly spat the gum into Julia's palm. She screwed up her face, thinking about it for a moment, before looking down her nose at Julia in the way she did.

"Nope," she said firmly. "Your boyfriend dragged Richard off before he got a chance."

"He's not my boyfriend," Julia corrected her as she tied her apron around her waist. "Although I do need to talk to him."

"Are you going to ask him on that date?"

"He already asked me again," Julia said, a smile spreading across her face, but then quickly vanishing when she remembered what day it was. "It's tonight!"

"Oh, please," Jessie said, rolling her eyes as she walked through the beads into the kitchen. "A moment while I vomit."

She let the excitement spread through her for a minute while Jessie was in the kitchen. She bit into her lip, wondering if she had anything suitable for a date in the back of her wardrobe.

Agatha Frost

CHAPTER 11

"Close your eyes," Sue demanded as she moved towards Julia with a small makeup brush. "Stop fidgeting!"

"It tickles," Julia said. "How much longer is this going to take?"

"Miracles don't happen without a lot of praying," Sue mumbled as she took a step back from Julia. "Needs more wing."

Julia attempted to look in the mirror that Sue had been blocking with her body since insisting on doing Julia's makeup. She had foolishly called her sister to ask for some advice on what she should wear, so when Sue showed up at her door ten minutes later clutching a trunk filled with more makeup than Julia knew what to do with, she instantly regretted calling her sister.

"Barker isn't going to be able to resist you when he sees you," Sue said, clearly pleased with her handiwork. "I've never seen you look so feminine."

"I don't know if that was a compliment or an insult."

"Both," Sue said. "Open your eyes and look at me."

Julia did as she was told. Her lids felt heavy under the weight of the eye shadow Sue had been precisely applying for the last twenty minutes, as did the rest of her face. She felt like she was wearing a mask; something she wasn't at all used to. She wasn't opposed to a little mascara or lipstick every now and then, but it wasn't practical to apply a full face of makeup before baking in the morning.

"Barker has seen me before," Julia said, trying her best to look past her sister to the mirror. "He knows exactly what I look like."

Lemonade and Lies

"There's nothing wrong with a little enhancement," Sue said as she dug in her trunk for more makeup. "A little highlight and I think we're done."

"I don't think my face can take anymore."

"It's the *final* touch. I promise. It'll just bring the whole thing together."

Sue swirled a clean brush in a compact of sparkly powder, which kicked up a small cloud of glittery dust. She dusted the powder on her cheeks, nose and cupids bow until she seemed satisfied that she had done her absolute most to make Julia look presentable for her date. When she was done, she stepped back, a proud grin spreading from ear to ear.

"You look like you're going to cry," Julia mumbled out of the corner of her mouth, scared to move in case the mask fell off.

"You look beautiful!" Sue said, clasping her hands together under her chin. "Oh, Julia. You look *so* beautiful."

Sue stepped to the side to finally let Julia see what she had done. Squinting in the dim light of her bedroom, Julia moved closer to her dressing table mirror. Her heart rate doubled in an instant.

"I look – I look-,"

"Beautiful!"

"*Like a clown!*" Julia cried, moving even closer to the mirror. "I don't even look like myself."

"That's the whole point!"

Julia closed one eye to get a better look at the black powder smoking up to her brow, unsure if it had been Sue's intention to make her look like a panda. Her cheeks were striped silver, pink and brown, bringing to mind Neapolitan ice-cream.

"I look like The Joker!" Julia moaned, pulling apart her sticky, red lips. "I look like a *clown!*"

"It'll look better when I've finished your hair," Sue said, already twisting Julia's wavy hair around the barrel of a curling iron. "Trust me."

Julia sat back in the chair and stared at her reflection, and for a moment she almost did submit to her sister's pruning. The heat of the curling iron sizzling against her scalp snapped her to her senses, and she sprang forward and out of the chair.

"This isn't me!" Julia said, clutching the small burn on the back of her head. "I'm sorry, Sue, but this isn't me."

Leaving her sister, Julia opened her bedroom door and walked through to the sitting room, where Jessie was flicking through the TV guide and drawing moustaches on the women. Julia needed an opinion she could trust, and she trusted Jessie's without question.

"Jessie?" Julia asked, resting her hands on her hips. "How do I look?"

Jessie mumbled her acknowledgment of Julia's presence but continued to perfect her moustache on a soap star's upper lip. Her tongue poked thoughtfully out of the corner of her mouth as she assessed her handiwork. Julia cleared her throat, and Jessie's head snapped up.

"Oh my God," Jessie spluttered loudly, not even trying to hold back her laughter. "What did she *do* to you?"

That was all Julia needed to hear. She turned on her bare heels and marched back into her bedroom.

"It's too much," Julia said as she looked around for her makeup wipes. "I have twenty minutes to look like myself before Barker is outside of my cottage."

"*Julia!*" Sue cried, pouting like she did whenever she didn't get her own way. "I've spent an hour working on that!"

Julia spotted the face wipes under her handbag on the corner of her dressing table, which was now cluttered with Sue's makeup. Julia couldn't believe all of those products were now smeared on her face. She had always wondered what she would look like under heavy makeup, and now that she knew, it wasn't something she would be doing again.

Julia reached out for the makeup wipes, but so did Sue. The sisters wrestled like girls a quarter of their age while Jessie snickered in the doorway.

"Let go!" Julia groaned, tugging hard on the makeup wipes.

Sue did let go of the wipes, but the force of it sent Julia falling back. She reached out for the dressing table to catch her, but her fingers closed around the soft leather of her tiny handbag. The bag followed her, and its contents fell to the ground, surrounding her. Jessie stopped laughing and helped Julia up off the ground, but Julia was already pulling out a wipe to clear her face.

"What's this?" Sue mumbled as she gathered up Julia's things.

Julia looked out of one of her eyes as she wiped the other. Sue was staring down at the page of suspects in Julia's small notepad.

"Dad? Katie?" Sue read aloud, turning around before Julia could snatch the notepad out of her hands. "Sally, Richard, Joanne and Terry? What is this, Julia?"

"Murder suspects," Jessie said, rolling her eyes. "Isn't it obvious?"

"Julia?"

"Like Jessie said," Julia mumbled quietly as she pulled a second wipe from the packet, the first looking like it had just been ran through the dirt. "Suspects for Charles Wellington's murder."

"You've been investigating, haven't you?" Sue sighed, her eyes soaking in every detail of Julia's notes on the next page. "Why can't you just leave this to the professionals?"

"Julia's the smartest woman I know," Jessie spat out, looking angrily down her nose at Sue. "She's better than any copper."

Julia smiled gratefully through the mirror at Jessie, who took a sheepish step back as though surprised by her own words.

"I don't think Dad did it," Julia said. "I just haven't crossed his name out yet. He told me he was out in the grounds when Charles was pushed, but Katie told me they were together in Dad's study. Dad found Katie in his study drinking whiskey, but I suspect that was after Charles was pushed. Katie's feet match the size of the boot prints found at the scene of the crime."

"Boots?" Sue cried, shaking her head and tossing the notepad on the cluttered dressing table. "How do you know all of this?"

"I ask the right questions."

"And the other names?" Sue appeared in the mirror behind Julia as she wiped off the last of the eyeliner surrounding her lashes. "Why do you suspect them?"

Sue sat on the edge of the bed and stared at her. Julia could tell Sue was trying to appear angry, even a little concerned, but the curiosity was also there. If Julia didn't tell her, she knew Sue would rack her brains all night to piece things together. Julia almost didn't want to say a word. She wanted Sue to know what it felt like to have pieces of a puzzle swirling around in her brain.

"Sally and Richard were both at the garden party when Charles was pushed out of the window, but they weren't with the rest of us," Julia started as she examined her fresh face, glad to see herself again. "We all saw Richard fight with Charles, but we didn't see him actually strike Charles. When I saw Richard yesterday, his knuckles were cut, but the cuts weren't fresh. Sally told me when she arrived at Peridale Manor, she saw Richard in a state and he wanted to get out of there in a hurry. I don't know for sure, but I think we can all assume that Sally and Charles were having an affair, and that's why Richard attacked Charles."

Lemonade and Lies

"So you're saying Richard found Charles after the fight, hit him, and then tossed him out of the window?" Sue asked, edging closer to the end of Julia's bed.

"Not necessarily," Julia said as she applied a generous amount of her favourite moisturiser. "That's the obvious theory, but I have a feeling Sally is lying to me about something. She seems scared of Richard."

"Do you think she saw him push Charles?"

"Or he saw her and he's covering for her?" Jessie offered, sitting next to Sue. "You're right, she *did* look scared of him, but wouldn't you if somebody knew you had committed murder?"

"Exactly," Julia said, the smile in the mirror telling her that they were on the same page.

"And the others?" Sue asked. "Joanne and Terry? I thought Terry was just the builder?"

"Do you remember what Gran said about seeing Terry in the manor around the time Charles was pushed?" Julia said, turning in her chair to face them both. "I spoke to Joanne. She told me they were both in the garden waiting for Katie to bring everybody to see the pool being dug."

"Do you think she's lying?" Sue asked, her eyes widening in shock.

"She could be," Julia said, nodding in agreement. "Or she just remembered wrong. They weren't suspects until earlier today. I went to Peridale Manor to talk to Dad and I saw them both in the builder's work cabin, so I went to speak to them to ask some questions, but I overheard them arguing before I had a chance."

"About the murder?" Jessie asked, her brows furrowing. "That's a bit of a stupid thing to do."

"Not quite," Julia said, shrugging softly. "It's open to interpretation. Joanne told Terry it was a good thing that Charles was dead and that they were in a bad place financially. She accused Terry of getting them into a mess, and that he had to sort it out."

"Terry has a gambling problem," Sue said, snapping her fingers together. "Neil told me he had to throw Terry out of the library for using the computers to gamble. He said he was in there every single day placing huge bets and then getting really angry when he lost money. Neil didn't feel right about it, so he approached him and told him not to come in if he was going to use the library computers for that. He didn't exactly ban him, but he as good as did."

"That explains the money troubles," Jessie said,

looking from Sue to Julia. "And why Joanne would say she is glad that man is dead. If they are really broke, getting that spa job would be a pretty big deal, wouldn't it?"

"But what does that have to do with Charles?" Sue asked.

"Aren't you listening?" Jessie asked with a roll of her eyes. "Charles wanted to stop the house turning into a stupid spa. If he succeeded, that broke builder and his missus would lose their contract and most of the money with it. With the Wellington dude out of the way, Terry gets to finish his work and make the money."

"It wasn't that obvious," Sue mumbled, looking from Jessie to Julia, hoping in vain that Julia hadn't already figured it out too. "It does make sense though."

"I'll know more when I speak to them both," Julia said, turning back to the mirror to apply a light coat of mascara.

"Or you could just leave it to Detective Inspector Brown and his team," Sue said. "They've probably already gotten this far."

"Perhaps," Julia said, knowing they hadn't. "But where's the fun in that?"

Jessie smirked at her in the mirror. Julia felt like

she was getting closer and closer to figuring out the truth, but for now, she pushed it out of her mind so she could focus on her date with Barker. After applying a subtle berry lipstick, she climbed into one of her nicer dresses and some kitten heels.

"How do I look?" Julia asked, standing in front of Jessie and Sue.

"Like you always do," Sue said, the disappointment loud and clear.

"Good," Julia said, turning to the mirror to run her fingers through her naturally messy curls. "That's exactly what I was going for."

CHAPTER 12

Peridale's only restaurant, The Comfy Corner, was Julia's favourite place to eat when she wasn't at her café, so when they pulled into the small backstreet it was nestled on, her face lit up.

"I hope you don't mind keeping it local," Barker said as he pulled up outside of the small restaurant. "I don't know the area too well yet and this place came highly recommend from the boys at the station."

"It's perfect," Julia said, looking up at its twinkling sign. "They have the best carbonara this side of Italy."

Barker got out and walked around the car. Julia took the opportunity to look in the visor mirror. She wasn't a vain woman, but she also didn't want to have lipstick on her teeth. Before she could open the door, Barker pulled it open and offered his hand.

"Thank you," Julia said, getting out of the car without using his offer of assistance.

"Have I mentioned how beautiful you look yet?" Barker asked as he shut the car door behind her. "Because you do."

"Twice."

"Oh," Barker said, nodding his head. "Sorry. Can you tell I'm nervous?"

"A little," Julia admitted. "You don't need to be nervous of me, Detective."

"Are you sure?"

Julia chuckled softly and walked towards the restaurant's door. She found it endearing that Barker was nervous about their date. It meant he cared, and she liked that. She couldn't ever imagine her soon-to-be ex-husband, Jerrad, being nervous around her. He had always been collected and lacking in emotion to the point of being robotic.

"Evening, Julia," Mary Potter, the owner of the small restaurant said. "Are you here for your big date with Barker?"

"Word does travel fast," Julia mumbled under her breath, wondering how many people her gran had called that afternoon. "Table for two, please."

"The candles are already burning," she said with a soft wink. "Follow me."

Barker's hand settled into the small of Julia's back as they walked across the restaurant. It took her so much by surprise, her entire body turned rigid. It had been so long since a man had touched her, she had almost forgotten how nice it could feel.

"Perfect table for a date," Mary said when she stopped at a table tucked away in an alcove, and out of view from the rest of the restaurant. "We call it lover's corner. Can I get you any drinks?"

"Dry white wine," Julia said as she sat in the chair Barker had just pulled out for her.

"Water for me," Barker said, patting his car keys. "Better safe than sorry."

Mary nodded and shuffled over to the bar. She was a gentle woman in her sixties, but she was also notoriously nosey. Most people in Peridale were, but Mary was nosier than most. Nothing got past the woman. She seemed to know things about people that were so secretive, villagers had accused her on more than one occasion of hiding secret recording devices around the restaurant. Julia didn't believe the rumour, but it was the reason her gran boycotted the place.

"It's quite charming in here," Barker said, looking around the comforting stone and oak interior. "You don't get places like this in the city."

"It used to be a pub. Dates back centuries," Mary said as she shuffled back with their drinks. "These walls could tell you some stories. Each brick tells a tale."

Mary set their drinks on the table, along with the menus she had nestled under her arm. She recommended the Peridale Pie, as she always did, and shuffled back to the bar.

"What's a Peridale Pie?" Barker whispered over the top of his menu.

"It's basically a cheese and onion pie with curry spices thrown in for good measure," Julia whispered back. "Mary's husband, Todd, is the chef and he's rather eccentric."

"Certainly sounds interesting," Barker mumbled as he looked through the leather bound menu. "As does everything on here. I never thought I'd see a

Tennessee burger next to a beef wellington."

"It's rather eclectic, but everything is delicious."

They looked over the menu in silence for a couple of minutes and Julia settled on chicken liver pâté on toast for her starter, and the spaghetti carbonara for her main. Sue had warned her against eating messy food on the date, but Julia knew if a little carbonara sauce on her chin scared away a man, he wasn't worth keeping.

"Speaking of Wellington," Barker said. "I hear you were at Peridale Manor again yesterday."

Julia had assumed mentioning the case was off limits for their date, but now that Barker had brought it up, she wasn't going to dance away from the subject.

"I wanted to establish my father's alibi," Julia said. "Which I suppose you already know doesn't marry up with his wife's?"

"I do," Barker said with a quick nod as he snapped the menu shut. "What the heck, I'll try the Peridale Pie! Oxtail soup for starters too."

Julia closed her menu and glanced around the edge of the alcove. Mary was talking to her husband. She didn't doubt for a moment that they were discussing their date.

"I'm surprised you're not telling me to stay out

of things," Julia said after a sip of wine.

"I've come to realise that no matter what I say you'll do what you want. I like that about you. You're a strong woman."

"Most men don't like a strong woman."

"I'm not most men."

"I've realised that, Detective," Julia said, holding back her smile. "You are certainly different than the usual Peridale men."

"Do you know that for a fact?" Barker asked, his eyes twinkling darkly in the soft candlelight. "Any skeletons in the closet that I should know about?"

Julia became flustered, but she was saved having to mention her divorce when Mary came to take their order. She fumbled with her hair, tucking it behind her ear. The last thing she wanted to talk about was her divorce.

Mary took their orders, complimenting them on their choices, and also recommending a dessert if they still had room at the end. When she hobbled away, Julia was glad Barker didn't immediately pick up where they had left off.

"Do you think your step-mother is capable of murder?" Barker asked, leaning across the table, his lips obscured by the flickering flame of the tall candle. "Off the record."

"Is she your prime suspect?"

"Isn't she yours?" Barker asked, his brows creasing as though there was no other option. "I'm assuming you've figured out her foot size matches, and we all saw her put on the boots."

"It certainly seems to make sense."

"But?" Barker sat back, a grin forming.

"There is no but," Julia said, shrugging softly. "I just like to keep all options open. When a cake isn't working, I don't throw in the first ingredient I can think of. I take my time, assess the flavours and really make sure I'm adding the right thing. Sometimes that first thought is right, but more often than not, it's wrong. You can always add, but you can't take away."

"So you don't think she did it?"

"I didn't say that."

"Well, obviously there's Richard," Barker offered, leaning back into the flame of the candle, appearing to revel in talking the case over with Julia. "I've interviewed him twice now, but aside from attacking Charles, there's nothing else. Sally says she was with him at the time of the murder."

"She did?" Julia said, a brow unintentionally arching. "She told me something different."

"You've interviewed her?"

"I'm making her wedding cake," Julia said innocently. "Which she cancelled, and then re-ordered. They're back together now, but when they were broken up, she told me she went to Peridale Manor to talk to him, saw him, then he left."

"She told me they both left and went home," Barker said, his eyes narrowing to dark slits. "Why would she lie?"

Before Julia could offer her theory, Mary appeared with Julia's chicken liver pâté on toast, and Barker's oxtail soup. They thanked her and she vanished again. They both started to eat, but Julia could feel Barker itching to discuss further.

"I sensed she was lying to me," Julia offered after cutting her toast slice in two. "Either story could be true, or both lies."

"She's hiding something. I just don't know what," Barker said before blowing a spoonful of his hot soup. "Do you think either of them did it?"

"Possibly," Julia said with a nod. "Have you considered Joanne and Terry Lewis?"

"Who?"

Julia contained her smirk. She took her time popping a piece of the pâté-covered toast into her mouth. She chewed slowly, enjoying Barker watching her intently as he messily slurped his soup.

Lemonade and Lies

"Terry Lewis is the contractor working on the spa conversion," Julia said when she felt she had left him to sweat it out long enough. "Joanne is his wife."

"Why do you suspect them?"

"They're having money troubles, and Joanne lied about Terry's alibi. She told me her and her husband were in the garden at the time of the murder but my gran saw and spoke to him in the manor."

"Have you ever considered your gran did it?" Barker teased. "Normally I wouldn't imagine a lady in her eighties throwing a fully grown man out of a window, but she's something else. She scares me. Did you know she was running an illegal poker club?"

"It's now a book club," Julia said with a small chuckle. "They're reading Fifty Shades of Grey."

Barker choked on his soup, his cheeks burning red. He dabbed at his lips with a cotton napkin and stared at Julia as if expecting her to say she was joking.

"This village is certainly colourful," Barker said as he resumed his soup. "Who do you think did it?"

"It's too soon to say," Julia said honestly. "It's not even been a week yet. There are still things to be discovered."

"Such as?"

Before Julia could answer, Mary reappeared to ask them both how their food was at the very moment they were mid-chew. They nodded and mumbled their satisfaction, turning down Mary's offer of drink refills. She knowingly smiled at Julia and mouthed something that looked like '*he's so handsome*' before leaving them once again.

"We still don't know what was taken from that display plinth next to the window," Julia said. "I feel like it holds the key to finding out the truth."

"I was sure that was unrelated until this morning," Barker said after taking his last mouthful of soup. "The autopsy came back and the coroner said there was a wound so severe on Charles' head that it was very likely he was dead before he was even thrown out of the window."

Julia finished the last of her pâté, but she didn't say anything. Barker looked at her, confused for a moment, before rolling his eyes and smiling.

"But you already knew that, right?" Barker asked.

"Didn't it strike you as odd that Charles was completely silent as he fell from the window?" Julia asked. "Have you ever heard of somebody silently falling to their death? Whatever was taken, I'm sure it was heavy enough to kill a man."

"Katie and your father are saying they can't remember what was there," Barker said with a sigh as he leaned back in his chair and glanced around the restaurant. "I don't believe it for a second."

"It is possible they don't remember," Julia offered, unsure if she believed her own words. "It's a big house."

"The one person who would know can't even speak. I tried to interview Vincent, but I got nothing."

Before Julia could tell him there was one person in the manor that would know what had been taken, Mary appeared to take away their plates. Instead of shuffling straight away, she lingered for a moment.

"Are you still selling that shortbread of yours?" Mary asked Julia, her eyes closing as she licked her lips. "My Todd is Scottish and he said you make it better than any Scot he's met. Simply divine."

"It's still there," Julia said. "I'll bring you some up soon."

"You're such a sweet girl," Mary gushed, turning to Barker. "You've got yourself a good one here, Detective."

Barker smiled and blushed again, but he didn't

say anything. When Mary finally left them alone, it seemed both of them had forgotten what they were talking about.

"So," Barker said, exhaling heavily. "Any men in Peridale I should watch out for slashing my tyres after they find out I've taken you on a date?"

Julia nervously laughed, her lips wobbling but unable to speak. She glanced around the alcove, hoping Mary was on her way back to cause further distraction, but she wasn't. Julia turned back to Barker, who was looking at her expectantly. Just when she was about to spill the beans about her estranged husband, Barker's phone rang loudly in his pocket.

"Bloody hell," Barker cried as he fumbled for his phone. "I told them not to call me. Do you mind?"

"Not at all," Julia said, relieved and grateful for the timing. "It could be important."

Barker excused himself and walked across the restaurant, only answering the phone when he was out of earshot from Julia. She watched as he paced up and down the empty restaurant, ducking out of the way of the low beams as he went. It hadn't gone unnoticed how handsome he looked in his dinner suit.

"That was work," Barker said, his voice grave

and his eyes so wide, Julia knew what was coming. "There's been a break-in at Peridale Manor. I'm going to have to go."

"I'm coming with you," Julia said before tossing back the rest of her wine and standing up. "And don't argue, Detective. I'm technically family so you can't stop me. If you don't take me with you, I'll call a taxi."

For a moment Julia thought Barker might protest and insist that she stay and eat her dinner, or go home, but he didn't. He sighed, and turned on his heels to head straight for the door. At that moment, Mary pushed through a door holding spaghetti carbonara in one hand and Peridale Pie in the other.

"We're going to have to go," Barker said apologetically, pulling a red fifty-pound note out of his wallet. "Keep the change."

Julia apologised as she passed Mary. Even the smell of her favourite dish at The Comfy Corner didn't tempt her to stay. She heard Mary mumble something about '*young love*' as she headed back into the kitchen.

CHAPTER 13

The drive up to Peridale Manor was a silent one. When they pulled up outside, there was already a police car on the scene. They both jumped out of the car the second Barker put his handbrake in place.

The front door was open, and Katie, Brian and two officers were talking in the grand entrance. Katie was hysterically chattering in a luminous pink nightie while Brian held her, and the two young officers attempted to write down what she was saying.

"Julia?" Brian mumbled, his forehead furrowing. "What are you doing here?"

"I was with Detective Inspector Brown," she said. "There was no time to take me home."

Her father nodded, seeming to accept this without question. His pale face and blank expression didn't go unnoticed. It was the same face Julia had seen at the garden party after discovering Charles' body. Was it the face of a man who knew he was holding onto a guilty woman?

"Mrs. Wellington," Barker said, stepping in front of the two bemused officers. "I'm going to need you to calm down and tell me what exactly happened here tonight."

"Wellington-*South*," she bumbled through her tears. "There was a man. A man upstairs!"

"A man?" Barker asked, glancing suspiciously to Julia. "Can you be more specific?"

"A masked man upstairs," Katie said angrily through her sobs. "I was c-c-coming out of the bathroom and I saw a masked m-m-man all dressed in black. I screamed, and he ran away."

Barker looked even more suspiciously to Julia

out of the corner of his eye. It was obvious he didn't believe her. Julia wasn't sure if she did either. The description of a masked burglar almost seemed cartoonish.

"And did anyone else see this masked man?" Barker asked, turning to roll his eyes at the officers. "Anyone to corroborate your story?"

"*Story?*" Katie shrieked, her voice echoing in every corner of the manor. "It's not a *story*, it's the *truth!*"

"Did you see this man?" Barker asked, turning his attention to Julia's father.

Brian awkwardly looked down at his hysterical wife, but he shook his head. Julia noticed his grip on her loosen.

"Was anything taken?" Barker asked, pinching between his brows.

"Well – *no*," Katie said. "I don't think so. I think I scared him off."

"And this burglar was alone? They didn't put up a fight?"

"They just ran down the stairs and out of the front door."

Barker audibly sighed, clearly frustrated with Katie. Julia knew exactly what he was thinking without needing to ask; she was thinking it too. It wasn't common for burglars to act alone, especially in such big houses, and she also knew they didn't tend to be unarmed or scared of a shrieking woman in her silk nightie.

Barker turned and started whispering with the two officers while Katie buried her mascara-streaked face in her husband's chest. Brian didn't put his arms around her, instead just staring into space. Julia realised nobody was paying her any attention, so she slipped away unseen and practically sprinted up the staircase.

Julia saw exactly what she wanted to see on the top step; the display plinth was no longer empty. A white marble bust was sitting on the display plinth. Just to be sure, she pulled her phone out of her handbag to check the picture she had taken on the day of the murder.

"Detective Inspector," Julia called over her shoulder as she took a second photograph of the plinth. "You might want to come and see this."

Barker and the two officers ran up the staircase, joining her in front of the bust.

"Look," Julia showed Barker the image of the missing marble bust on her phone, then she flicked to the one she had just taken in the exact same position. "*Earl Philip Wellington*. Born 1798, died

1865."

Katie and Brian joined them in the crowded hallway and they all stared at the bust.

"That's my great-great-great-great-grandfather," Katie mumbled through her sobs. "He built this manor."

"When I asked you what had been taken from this plinth, you claimed not to have remembered," Barker said sternly, the vein in his temple throbbing brightly. "Tonight when you claim a man broke into your home, this bust is suspiciously returned. As you know from my phone call earlier this afternoon, your brother was potentially killed by a blow to the head with a heavy object."

As Barker explained the situation to Katie, Julia leaned into the bust, detecting the unmistakable scent of heavy bleach. Whoever had returned the bust had made sure to clean it thoroughly first. She doubted even the best forensics team would be able to find a speck of blood or a fingerprint on the sterile marble.

"I just forgot," Katie protested, looking to Brian, her unnaturally shaped brows dashing up her shiny forehead. "It's a big house. You can't *prove* anything! You can't *prove* that bust was taken!"

"I have pictures," Julia said, stepping forward

with her phone in her hands.

Barker's hand closed in around her arm and he pulled her back before she could turn the phone around. He leaned into her ear, his breath hot on her cheek.

"If anybody finds out I let you investigate a crime scene before I shut it down, I'll be in deep trouble," Barker whispered darkly.

Julia gritted her jaw as she looked down at the picture of the empty plinth on her phone. She was instantly offended that she wasn't allowed to show what she had found for the sake of Barker not getting in trouble at the station, but she relented and stepped back, mumbling that she had made a mistake.

"See, you *can't* prove it!" Katie said, grinning like a mad Cheshire cat. "You can't prove the bust was taken. It's your word against mine. We say it wasn't taken. Don't we, babe?"

Katie turned to Brian, who didn't say a word. He gulped hard, a cold sweat breaking out on his forehead, trickling down the side of his deeply tanned and lined face.

"Babe?" Katie asked, less sure.

Julia might not have been her father's biggest fan, but she didn't like seeing him in such a moral dilemma. She stepped forward again as she dropped her phone back into her handbag.

"There's one person who will be able to confirm if the bust was taken or not," Julia said, wanting to take the heat away from her father.

"My father can't even speak!" Katie cried. "The man had a stroke less than a month ago!"

Julia stepped to the side of Katie and looked straight down the dark hallway to the woman peeking through a door, and had been ever since Julia had called for Barker.

"Hilary?" Katie laughed, but her expression soon turned dark.

"Officer Galbraith, I want you to hold Katie in the kitchen," Barker said, his voice professional and calm. "I have a witness to speak with."

"You *can't* do this!" Katie shrieked.

"Calm yourself Mrs. Wellington, or I'll have you cuffed," Barker ordered, his finger in the woman's face.

"It's Wellington-South," she muttered, less confident this time. "Wellington-*South*."

Julia's father's study was a dark room lined with bookshelves bursting with hefty hardback volumes. The room was windowless and claustrophobic, each book adding to the suffocation. As Hilary carefully walked across the room to the chair in front of the desk where Barker was sitting behind the dimly lit lamp, Julia knew why he had picked this room above any other.

Hilary sat in the chair in front of the desk, her posture composed, her lips pursed, and her wiry grey hair tightly scraped into a taut bun at the back. Even though Julia was standing at the back of the room, she could imagine Hilary's darkly lined eyes bulging in the soft glow of the lamp.

"Hilary," Barker started, leaning back in the chair and resting his fingers on his chest. "Do you have a last name, Hilary?"

"That's none of your business," she said firmly, her voice breathy but stern. "I haven't done a thing wrong."

"Nobody is saying you have," Barker said, quickly leaning into the light. "Unless you want to tell me something?"

Julia held back laughter. She knew Barker was trying to scare Hilary into slipping up, but Julia found his interrogation techniques more comical than frightening. Hilary seemed to think the same because she busied herself with adjusting the hem of her skirt.

"Hilary Boyle," the housekeeper said reluctantly. "What does any of this nasty business have to do with me? I've already told you I was in the kitchen at the time of the murder and I have a dozen waitresses and waiters to tell you the same. I saw the poor boy fall from the window from within the house."

"I don't doubt that," Barker said, looking up at the ornate ceiling before looking right back at her, his eyes narrow and firm. "Did you know Charles well?"

"I've known that boy since the day he was born," Hilary said, her voice not wavering. "I knew he was trouble from the first time I heard him cry."

"And Katie?"

Hilary wavered for the first time. She shifted in her chair, glancing over her shoulder at Julia. Julia was still surprised Barker had let her sit in on the interview, but she was the only one he had allowed. She had promised not to say a word.

"She's just as bad," Hilary said softly. "If not worse. A rude, insolent child. If Mr Wellington hadn't lost his tongue, he would tell you the same."

"I gather you've been here for a long time?" Barker asked, his fingers drumming heavily on the desk. "Long enough to know the layout pretty well?"

"I know this house like the back of my hand,"

Hilary said, pride loud and clear in her voice. "Like it's a part of my own skin."

"And you clean it quite regularly?"

"Every single day."

"Dusting?"

"I beg your pardon?"

"Do you dust, Mrs. Boyle?" Barker asked, leaning closer into the light, shadows dripping down his chiselled face. "Ornaments, for example?"

"Are you questioning my credentials as a cleaner, Detective?" Hilary asked harshly. "Because I assure you, I'm the best this village has to offer! And it's *Miss* Boyle to you. I never married."

"I apologise, Miss Boyle," Barker said, holding his hands up. "I didn't mean to offend, I just wanted to check you knew this house and its contents. Have you noticed anything go missing recently?"

Hilary shifted once again in her seat, telling them both exactly what they wanted to know. She glanced over her shoulder at Julia before looking down to continue adjusting the hem of her skirt.

"I assume you're talking about the bust?" she asked. "I did wonder about that. It's not my place to ask. I assumed the brat had sold it to try and cover some of the costs of her silly idea to turn this fine manor into a tacky spa. You hear whisperings if you listen hard enough, and the money isn't flowing like it used to."

"You didn't think to mention this absent bust to the police?" Barker asked.

"Why *would* I?" Hilary snapped, clearly offended. "What does this have to do with *anything*?"

"That's confidential, Miss Boyle," Barker said firmly. "When was the last time you saw the bust?"

"Ten minutes ago when you dragged me from my room," Hilary said, resting her hands on the table and matching Barker's pose by leaning into the light. "I was just about to go to bed, you know. It's silver polishing tomorrow, and I like to get it done before breakfast. I assume, however, that you're asking when was the last time I saw the bust *before* I noticed it had gone missing. It was the morning of the garden party."

"Are you sure?"

"Of course I am sure," Hilary cried, the offence louder in her voice than ever before. "Are you trying to insinuate that I am going senile? I'm as sharp as a knife and as bright as a bulb, I'll have you know. That morning, Katie was being extra brat-like and she made me clean the entire house from top to bottom. I specifically remember because I forgot my marble polish and I had to run back downstairs to get it. Vincent – *I mean* – Mr. Wellington is very specific about cleaning things with the right equipment. He is very proud of this manor and its history. Before I could even get back upstairs to clean it, Katie sent me out to the garden with lemonade for the builders, and it never got done."

Having heard all he needed to, Barker thanked Hilary and stood up. He buttoned up his dinner jacket and headed straight for the door.

"You're going to arrest her, aren't you?" Julia asked.

Barker didn't say a word. He opened the door and walked swiftly across the entrance hall to the kitchen. Hilary stood up and adjusted her skirt, gazing menacingly at Julia. Seconds later, Katie's shrieks echoed throughout the manor, and Julia didn't need to look to know the two officers were dragging her towards the front door.

When Katie's cries grew more distant, Julia walked out of the study. First she saw Barker standing in the kitchen doorway talking quietly on his phone, then she saw her father standing at the top of the stairs, staring blankly down at the front door. He didn't protest, or say anything to help his wife, he just stared as though he was as mute as

Vincent. Even from her distance, Julia noticed a tear rolling down his cheek as he turned away.

"Whose side are you on, girl?" Hilary asked bitterly as she walked slowly past Julia shaking her head. "You kids have no sense of loyalty these days."

Julia turned to Barker as he walked slowly across the hall towards her. He smiled uneasily at her, but she couldn't smile back.

"We did it," Barker said, letting out a relieved sigh. "How do you feel?"

"Not as pleased as I expected," Julia admitted, looking to the spot her father had been standing as Hilary reached the top of the stairs. "It feels so unresolved."

"The truth will come out," Barker reassured her, resting his hand on her shoulder. "Her alibi was the only one that didn't check out. She was in the house at the time her brother was murdered, and she is the only person with such an obvious motive. I'm sure when forensics get their hands on the bust, they're going to find her prints and his blood. I'm sorry this ruined our date."

"As first dates go, this one was certainly different," Julia said, enjoying the feeling of Barker's hand resting heavily on her shoulder, his thumb touching the exposed part of her collarbone. "I'll let

Lemonade and Lies

you take me home now, Detective."

CHAPTER 14

It rained again all day, but that didn't stop people coming into Julia's café to gossip. She took almost record takings from the residents who wanted somewhere to sit and talk about Katie's arrest. The rain seemed to help keep them there hours longer than usual, and by noon it was standing room only.

When Julia finally shooed the last customers out

of the café at the end of the day and flipped the sign, the forced smile dropped from her face and she rested her head against the door, completely exhausted. She hadn't been able to sleep much the night before because Katie's shrieking had rattled around her ears until the early hours. She was sure she only managed an hour of sleep before Jessie's head banging on the wardrobe door jolted her out of her exhausted slumber.

"You look knackered," Jessie said, letting out her own yawn as she started to clear away the messy tables. "I thought you would have slept better last night knowing that your step-mother who isn't your step-mother is behind bars."

Julia untied her apron and pulled it over her head, tossing it onto a table. She caught Jessie's yawn, and her mouth opened so wide she thought it was never going to close again. The bags under her eyes were practically ruched. All she could think of was her bed, however, there was somebody she wanted to visit before she could do that.

"Are you okay cleaning up on your own?" Julia asked, already grabbing her pink coat and umbrella from the hooks in the kitchen. "I'll lock the door. Just use the spare keys to let yourself out and lock up if I'm not back."

"Where are you going?" Jessie asked after dropping a pile of dishes into the hot soapy water she had just run.

"How do you feel about college?" Julia asked.

"College?" Jessie replied with a deep frown. "I wasn't any good at school. I failed all my exams."

"Joanne's son, Jamie, is on a building apprenticeship," Julia said as she pushed her arms through her coat. "He studies at college one day a week, but he works for the rest of the week. You're already doing that, so why not get qualified?"

Jessie screwed her up face before looking down her nose at Julia.

"You mean, like a certificate?" Jessie asked. "A real one?"

"As real as they come," Julia said, glad that Jessie wasn't dismissing it outright. "It'll look good for when your social worker visits if we're showing that you're settling into Peridale. This is just another way to do that."

The mention of her social worker stiffened Jessie in an instant, and her face turned bright red as though she had completely stopped breathing. Julia stared at her young lodger as she buttoned up her jacket, suddenly realising she hadn't heard from the social worker in a while.

"Yeah, whatever," Jessie said, spinning and picking up a dirty plate which she started to vigorously scrub.

"Joanne has a prospectus for the college so we'll have a look properly tonight," Julia said, grabbing her handbag and tossing it over her shoulder. "If you need anything, you have my mobile number."

Jessie nodded, her dark ponytail bobbing up and down. As she walked through the café towards the door, she wondered why Jessie was so scared of her social worker. When they had spoken on the phone, she had seemed like a pleasant lady, even if she had not sent out the paperwork she said she would.

Julia pushed up her umbrella the second she stepped outside, pulling it close to her head. Strong wind almost knocked her off her feet as she walked around the village green. The umbrella did little to protect her from being soaked by the sideways falling rain, which was tumbling so heavily it bounced off the road underfoot.

Julia was glad Joanne's cottage was only around the corner, nestled along with three other terraced cottages between The Cozy Corner and Peridale's tiny library. She hadn't realised how close the Lewis house was to the library, which made sense of Terry's gambling visits. She imagined Joanne had banned him from doing it in the house, driving him next door.

The houses were directly on the narrow winding road, meaning Julia had no protection from the rain as she stood and waited for somebody to answer the door. A car zoomed by, sending water cascading over her. A cold cry escaped her lips as the icy water soaked through to her figure, driving her knuckles harder into the thick door.

When the door finally opened, it was Jamie Lewis, not Joanne or Terry who answered.

"Is your mother home?" Julia asked, her teeth chattering as she clung desperately to her useless umbrella, her hands white and freezing.

"She's out shopping," Jamie mumbled, barely making eye contact with Julia.

"Will she be long?"

Jamie shrugged and looked over his shoulder to the roaring fire in the heart of the sitting room.

"Could I possibly come in to wait?" Julia said, forcing herself to smile. "I'm quite soaked through."

Jamie sighed, and Julia almost expected him to slam the door in her face, but he stepped to the side and let her in. Julia hurried in backwards, collapsing her umbrella as she went. Jamie closed the door behind her. For a moment she stood dripping on the doormat while she tried to catch her breath.

"Could I have something to warm me up?" Julia asked. "Some tea, perhaps?"

"Whatever," Jamie said with a shrug.

"Plop this in some boiling water," Julia said, pulling a soaked peppermint and liquorice tea sachet from her handbag. "Emphasis on the word *boiling*."

Julia's attempt at humour didn't crack a smile on the surly teenager's face. He snatched the teabag out of Julia's shaking fingers and lumbered off to the kitchen, leaving Julia to her own devices. She pulled off her coat, glad that her dress beneath was only wet at the back. Nestling on a footstool in front of the roaring fire, she hugged her body as the warmth surged through her frozen flesh.

Jamie returned, practically tossing her tea onto the side table next to her, splashing and soaking a stack of letters. Julia's eyes instantly honed in on the red writing on the top one, which read '*DO NOT IGNORE. IMPORTANT*'. She didn't need x-ray vision to know it was probably a credit card or loan company chasing a debt.

Jamie threw himself onto the couch and picked up a controller to resume playing the fighting game he had been playing before Julia interrupted. She watched as the character on the screen shot a man three times at short range, no doubt controlled by Jamie. She looked at the teenager, who didn't seem phased by the gore on screen. Julia wondered if Jessie had grown up in a conventional and stable home, would she be interested in the same things as other teenagers?

"I've actually come to ask your mother about apprenticeships," Julia offered, attempting to add something to the awkward silence other than the boom of the gun. "She told me you're doing one in building."

"Construction," he corrected her, his thumbs tapping away on the controller.

"Do you enjoy it?"

Jamie shrugged heavily, staring ahead at the TV screen like a zombie. Julia wondered if the purple bags around his eyes were from a lack of sleep or just from staring at the screen for too long.

"Is today your day off?"

"They rang up and told us not to come in today," Jamie muttered, his attention firmly on the game. "Probably 'cause of the rain. Can't pour cement in the rain."

Jamie didn't seem to have heard about what had happened at Peridale Manor last night. She considered not telling him, but she was sure news would spread around the entire village by the end of the day.

"Katie Wellington-South was arrested last night," Julia said, picking up her mug and cupping it warmly in her hands. "For her brother's murder."

Jamie's thumbs stopped tapping and he paused the game. He turned to Julia, his brow stern.

"What?" Jamie snapped. "What does that mean?"

"It means that I don't know what is happening with the spa," Julia said. "I know your dad was relying on the work, but I don't know if the work will be there if she's convicted."

"My dad?" Jamie cried, his previously disinterested and quiet voice suddenly loud and full of passion. "You don't know the first thing about my dad, or what we're going through!"

"I'm sure you'll get another job," Julia offered, glancing to the letters on the side table. "I doubt this will change anything with your apprenticeship."

"My apprenticeship?" Jamie cried, tossing the controller onto the floor and suddenly standing up. "Do you think I *wanted* to do this stupid apprenticeship? I've only done it to help my dad. He needed the extra pair of hands for the spa job."

Julia put her tea back on the side table and stood

up, preparing herself to tell Jamie she would come back later. At that very moment, the door opened and Joanne hurried in, her hands full of shopping bags, and her short curly hair soaked to her scalp.

"Julia," she cried, her teeth chattering. "What a surprise."

Joanne looked from Julia to Jamie, who was still standing there, his breathing suddenly erratic. Julia wasn't sure what the teen was going to do, but he turned on his heels and stormed off up the narrow flight of stairs. A door slammed, shaking the cottage.

"Boys at that age," Joanne said with an awkward laugh. "Full of hormones and testosterone. I tell him that game isn't good for his moods."

Julia hurried over and took some of the shopping bags out of Joanne's hands, which she gratefully handed over.

"I stopped by to grab that college prospectus from you," Julia said as they walked through to the kitchen. "Jamie was kind enough to let me in out of the rain to dry off."

"Of course," Joanne said, slapping herself gently on the forehead after setting the bags down. "You know what, I've been so busy that I completely forgot. I'll go and grab it for you. It's in Jamie's bedroom, I think. That's if he's speaking to me."

Lemonade and Lies

Joanne let out another nervous laugh and rolled her eyes. Julia pondered if this was what she had in store if she fostered Jessie. With the sleepwalking suddenly occurring, she wondered what else was around the corner.

Leaving the kitchen, she walked back through to the sitting room to pick up her tea. Glancing to the staircase to make sure she was alone, she curiously picked up the top letter to see if the one underneath it appeared to be a debt letter. Julia was shocked when she reached the bottom of a pile of ten and they all appeared to be quite serious letters from various companies. Peridale's residents might not have wanted the spa, but she knew the Lewis family needed it. Her heart hurt to think Katie had offered them a way to solve their problems, and then taken it away just as quickly.

She remembered a period of financial difficulty early in her marriage when Jerrad had racked up a serious credit card debt and hidden the letters from her for over a year. When she found them stuffed in a box of cereal he knew she didn't like, she ripped open each envelope like a women possessed. The only reason she had opened the box was because it had passed its use by date. The rage and upset she had felt back then flared up inside of her again as she carried her cup through to the kitchen. She could only imagine how much worse things were for Joanne.

Jamie's bedroom door slammed again, yanking Julia out of her thoughts. She jumped, her heavy cup slipping from her still shaking fingers. It tumbled silently to the ground, much like Charles had from the window. With a loud smash, it split into three large pieces, ricocheting fragments of porcelain across the tiled floor. Glancing up at the kitchen ceiling, she expected to hear Joanne's footprints running down to her, but she didn't.

Making a mental note to confess her crime and offer to replace the mug, Julia opened the cupboard under the sink and fished the dustpan and brush from in between two large bottles of bleach. Bending down, she quickly brushed up the mess from the terracotta tiles, making sure to get right under the shopping bags.

Looking back up at the ceiling, she heard Joanne and her son bickering in low voices about something, no doubt about how many computer games he played.

Julia stepped over the shopping bags towards the bin with the cup fragments balanced in the dustpan. The front door opened and closed again, letting the sound of the wind rattle around the small cottage. She popped open the bin and glanced over her shoulder to see if somebody had just arrived, or if Jamie had just stormed out. Deciding it was none of her business either way, Julia turned her attention to the bin as she poured the broken cup in with the rubbish.

She almost released the bin pedal under her foot, but something black, set against something white caught her eyes. Glancing over her shoulder, she leaned in further, making out the shape of another giant bottle of bleach buried in the rubbish, and on top of it, the black thing appeared to be made of fabric. Reaching inside, she fished it out, shaking off the broken cup pieces as she did.

As she held the balaclava up in front of her face, her heart sunk to the pit her stomach. She stared into the soulless eyeholes, and they stared back, mocking her for getting things so wrong.

"Oh, Julia," she heard from behind her. "If only you had left things alone."

Dropping the balaclava, she turned just in time to see Terry Lewis holding the hot kettle over his head. It struck the side of Julia's skull, and she was unconscious before she hit the shopping bags.

CHAPTER 15

Julia was aware that she was travelling in a car before her eyes opened. She was also aware her ankles and wrists were tied before she tried to move them. Letting out a loud groan, she rolled her head against the headrest, a splitting pain piercing through her head as she watched the blurry streetlamps whiz by in the rain.

She thought she was dreaming, and any moment

Lemonade and Lies

Jessie's head banging or Mowgli jumping on her chest would wake her. Her eyelids were so heavy, but she tried to force them open as the orange lights blurred by. They suddenly stopped. She felt the tyres underneath her change from smooth road onto something bumpier. She realised that she was in danger.

She attempted to speak, to cry out, but all that left her mouth was a muffled groan. She bit down, her teeth landing in something soft. Was she gagged? Opening her eyes properly for the first time, she let out a terrified cry.

"Shut her up!" the driver commanded.

A hand vanished behind Julia's head, pulling the gag tighter into her mouth. Despite the pounding in her head, she turned to see Jamie Lewis sitting next to her in the back seat of the car. He blankly stared at her, emotionless and empty.

Julia shook her head and something hot and thick trickled down the side of her face. She attempted to lift her hands up to touch it, but Jamie yanked them back into her lap. She didn't need to put her fingers to the cut to know Terry's blow to her head had caused some serious damage. Her eyelids fluttered again, this time not from exhaustion, but from an intense wooziness. She tried to fight it, but against her own will, darkness claimed her.

Julia felt the rain on her skin before she opened her eyes. She felt the sensation of floating before she attempted to move her limbs. She assumed she was dead and entering the afterlife, but the pain in her head screamed out, letting her know that she was very much alive. She opened her eyes again and stared down into the darkness.

Frowning hard, she realised that she was being carried. She didn't know why, but the plod of the walk told her she was draped over Terry's shoulder. Instead of trying to make noise, she forced herself to stay silent, despite the intense pain and crippling fear.

"This has all gone too far," she heard Joanne hiss.

"She would have gone to the police," Terry said, and Julia could feel his words boom through his body and into hers. "We couldn't allow that. She wasn't just going to ruin our future, but our son's too. Is that what you want?"

"Of course not!" she snapped back.

"This wouldn't have happened if *you* hadn't been so useless," Terry said. "I'm tired of cleaning up *your* mess."

Julia waited for the person to reply, but they didn't. Without needing to open her eyes, she became aware of the presence walking two steps behind her. She wanted so desperately to see who it was, but she fought the urge to open her eyes.

"This is never going to work," Joanne moaned. "They're going to catch us."

"They're not," Terry bit back, his voice full of venom. "The bimbo is in jail and her other half is drowning his sorrows in a bottle of whiskey. He'll be asleep by now and I doubt anything is waking him. It's perfect."

"What about the old man?"

"He's had a stroke," Terry said with a dark laugh. "Even if he saw the whole thing, he wouldn't be able to say a word."

"Are you sure there's nobody else?"

"There's a housekeeper but she's old," Terry said, sounding irritated by Joanne's questions. "She'll be fast asleep."

"How are we even going to get in there?" Joanne asked, the worry loud and clear in her voice. "Oh, Terry, it's not too late."

"To do what?" he cried, his voice booming. "Hand ourselves in? Tell them the *truth* about what happened at the garden party? Is that what you want? *Huh*, Joanne? Is that what you *want*?"

"You know it isn't!"

"Then this is the only way," Terry said, readjusting his grip on Julia by tossing her in the air. "You know it is. Why did *you* let her into the house? You're an idiot, boy."

Julia realised the figure walking behind her was Jamie. Opening her eyes a fraction she looked down at his shoes. Heavy mud-covered work boots; size eight if she had to guess. Closing them again, she realised where they were going and what was likely about to happen.

"Get the key out of my pocket, Joanne," Terry instructed. "It's under her foot. Be careful not to wake her. If she's still out, she won't be able to make a sound."

"She's already awake," Jamie mumbled.

"What?" Terry cried, tossing Julia up so that she landed hard on his shoulder. "For how long?"

"Couple of minutes."

Terry turned, sending Julia into a spin. She opened her eyes and caught Joanne whizzing by. She didn't need to see Terry striking his son because she felt the back of his hand hitting Jamie's cheek through her body.

"This is all *your* fault!" Terry sneered. "You're pathetic."

Terry turned and started walking even quicker towards the house. She could hear Jamie sniffling into his sleeve, muffling his cries the best he could. They were the sobs of somebody who had learned to hide them.

"Get the key," Terry ordered again. "Come on! *Hurry up!* This needs to be *now!*"

Julia felt Joanne rummage under her restrained foot to pull something out of his pocket. Julia looked down and the gravel had turned to grass. They had reached Peridale Manor.

She heard the click of a lock and they left the rain. Just from the tiles, she could tell she was in the kitchen. It was cold, which meant the heating had been turned off for hours, likely making it the early hours of the morning.

The ground came from under Julia as Terry tossed her over his shoulder and slammed her onto the table as though she were a bag of sand. He gripped the front of her soaked dress and yanked her up into a sitting position so they were face to face. She stared into his dark eyes, the stubble around his mouth was peppered grey like the edges of Barker's hairline. She remembered their date and she started to uncontrollably sob and shake.

"Listen to me!" Terry said, shaking her shoulders. "*Shut up*, woman! Joanne, pass me that knife."

Joanne snatched up a large knife from the counter at the very moment a crack of white lightning pierced through the dark rain. It illuminated the kitchen, showing the madness in Terry's eyes and the fear in his wife and son's.

"Are you going to be good?" Terry asked, pressing the cold blade of the knife against Julia's face. "Or do I need to do this the painful way?"

Julia forced her cries to stop. In that moment, a sudden calmness fell over her as she stared into Terry's murky soul.

"Find me something to drink," he shot over his shoulder at Joanne. "I need something to take the edge off."

Joanne hurried over to the fridge, pulling its heavy doors open. The light flooded the kitchen. Julia could see Jamie pacing back and forth, sobbing silently and shaking out of control.

"There's only lemonade," she called.

"I need something *strong*!" Terry cried. "*Dammit*, woman. Get me some alcohol."

Joanne rummaged through every cupboard until

she found a bottle of cooking wine. That seemed to suit Terry perfectly. He pulled the cork out with his teeth, spat it out, and crammed the bottleneck into his mouth. Head tossed back, he gulped the dark wine like it was water, only stopping when he had drained every last drop. Eyes clenched, he bobbed his head forward as he panted for breath, his teeth and lips stained blood red.

"You're going to walk up those stairs," Terry said, pointing the knife in Julia's face, his large gut pressing against her knees. "And you're going to do it quietly, or else I kill every person in this house as they sleep. Do you understand?"

Julia nodded without thinking, making the dizziness return. She forced herself to stay with this world and not float through into the darkness between this and the next. She knew if she had any chance of walking out of the manor alive, she needed to stay focussed.

Terry quickly slid the knife down, making her think he was going to stab her. Instead, he sliced the restraints from her feet and dragged her off the table. Her ankles were weak and her head swirled from standing on her own for the first time. She caught her reflection in the dark kitchen window, the side of her face stained in scarlet.

"*Move*," he ordered, grabbing a fistful of the back of her dress and placing the knife dangerously close to her spine. "Come on. Walk."

Julia stumbled forward. She frantically looked to Jamie, but he was as with them as Julia had been during the second part of their car journey.

She took the steps as slowly as she could, trying to formulate a plan. She played up to her injury, staggering and grabbing the handrail. Terry's need for silence meant he wasn't going to hurt her until completely necessary, so as long as she kept her gagged mouth shut, she was keeping herself alive. She knew when she reached the top she would be walking towards the window like a pirate down the plank.

The moment Julia's shoe touched the top step, her body convulsed beyond her control. She wondered if the injury to her head was causing her to have a seizure, but she quickly realised it was out of sheer terror. She had stared down a blade before and expected death, but her life hadn't flashed before her eyes then. As she stared down at the polished mahogany floorboards, she saw everything before her. She thought of Sue, and her gran finding out she had been thrown from the same window as Charles Wellington. She thought of Jessie being cast back into the care system, and Mowgli back to the streets. She would never know what it would be like to finish a date with Barker, nor would she die divorced from the man she detested. Her café would gather dust, and her father would die an old man in prison after the Lewis family successfully framed the drunken man for her murder. The worse part was, she wondered if her father might even believe he did it. She didn't know how much of that whiskey he had drank, but she remembered how much he had drunk after her mother died, and it was a lot.

Thinking of her mother calmed her. It even sent a flicker of warmth through her body. She didn't know if she believed in a God, or in an afterlife, but the thought of possibly being reunited with her mother filled her with a swelling light. She had always known this day was coming and it had comforted her to think she might one day see her mother again, even if she hadn't expected it to be so soon.

The convulsing started again, and she looked up from the ground. She caught a man's eyes, but they weren't Terry's or Jamie's, they were much older and much blanker. She realised she was looking through a crack into Vincent Wellington's bedroom, where he was sitting under a blanket in his wheelchair in front of a silent TV. For a moment, she thought she saw those old vacant eyes widen, but before she could be sure, Terry pushed her on.

She turned her attention to the window. Its glass was fresh, but that wouldn't last long. Would death hurt? It wouldn't be like falling asleep, more like falling into a nightmare she wouldn't jolt from. She reconsidered if it was a nightmare, but it felt too real; the pain in her head felt too real.

Just thinking of the pain in her head made her ears burn with a deafening buzzing. She clenched her eyes and stopped, wanting to clutch her head. When she opened them, she realised the Lewis family could hear it too.

"What is that?" Joanne seethed through gritted teeth. "An alarm?"

"There wasn't an alarm when I put the bust back yesterday," Terry said.

Julia heard a door open, and then another. They all turned to see Brian and Hilary squinting into the dark, both disgruntled and half asleep.

"What the -," Brian mumbled over the alarm as he walked forward and flicked on a light. "*Julia?*"

Just hearing her father say her name immediately broke her. Tears flooded her cheeks, mixing with the blood and dripping through the gag so she could taste the mixture of iron and salt. Julia felt a renewed urge to survive this horrible night, so she ran in the only direction she could, towards the window.

Pushing her body up against the cold glass, she watched as Terry advanced on her brandishing his knife. Brian charged forward as Hilary stood screaming from behind her hands. Julia knew her father was never going to catch up to save her. She didn't want to fall onto the blade of a madman regretting so many years of her life, but she did. All she wanted was a hug from her dad.

"No!" a voice cried and a dark shadow appeared in front of her like a ghost, standing between her and the knife.

She heard a small whimper, but she didn't stick around to see what had happened. She leapt into her father's arms, her hands still restrained. Painful sobs escaped her throat and her father's lips pressed up against her forehead.

"It's all going to be okay," he whispered. "It's all going to be okay."

Julia realised she had been waiting to hear those words from him since the day her mother died.

Forcing back her tears, the sound of another's was drowning out the piercing alarm. She pulled away from her father to see Jamie and Terry stumbling towards the window. It looked as though they were hugging, but from the strained cries leaving Joanne's mouth, she knew something more serious had happened.

Jamie's eyes met her and they tensed, apologising in a way words couldn't. It was then she saw the blood dripping between them, and she realised exactly what had happened. Jamie had jumped in between her and the blade.

Julia noticed why it looked like they were hugging. Jamie was clutching onto his father's shirt as though the two were fused. With the strength of ten men, Jamie dragged his father with him through the window. The glass shattered and they both fell into the rain.

Unable to hold on anymore, Julia let the darkness take her as Joanne's screams rang throughout the whole of Peridale.

CHAPTER 16

J ulia's eyes shot open, instantly closing because of
the bright daylight. She forced them open again,
realising it wasn't daylight at all, but florescent
tubes in the hospital ceiling.

"She's awake!" she heard her gran cry. "Sue,
wake up! She's *awake*!"

Julia blinked hard, feeling like she had been
asleep for years. Against the beeping, she heard Sue's

groans as their gran woke her. Next to Sue, Jessie stirred from her sleep too.

"Huh?" Sue groaned, sitting up and rubbing her eyes. "What's happening?"

"She's awake!"

Sue, Jessie and Dot all rushed over to her side. Jessie clutched one hand, Sue clutched another and Dot rested her own hand on Julia's forehead, which she realised was bandaged up.

"How long have I been out?" she asked, her croakiness surprising her.

"Just a day," Dot said soothingly, her thumb rubbing over the bandages. "You gave us all quite a fright."

Julia remembered the blow to the head and everything that had happened following it. She remembered watching Terry and Jamie tumbling out of the window, and then fading into darkness in her father's arms. She knew it was all too bizarre to be a dream.

"Joanne?" she mumbled.

"She's been arrested," Sue said, squeezing Julia's hand. "You don't have to worry about them."

"The others?" she asked.

Sue looked to Jessie, who looked to Dot, who looked to Julia. None of them seemed to want to tell her what had happened.

"Terry died," Jessie said in a soft voice Julia didn't recognise. "Jamie is in intensive care."

"He survived?"

"He did it, Julia," Dot said. "Jamie struck Charles over the head. Joanne confessed everything."

"I know," Julia said. "I know why."

"It doesn't matter why," Sue said, squeezing Julia's hand again. "All that matters is you're safe, and that boy will leave this place in a box, or in handcuffs. Either way, he can't hurt you."

"No," Julia mumbled, coughing as she struggled for words. "He saved me. He stood in front of the blade."

They all looked from one to the other again, and she could tell they were wondering if she was under the influence of the heavy drugs she could feel pumping through her system. It was all so bizarre, she began to wonder that herself.

She was about to start explaining again, but the door creaked open and Barker walked through, clutching a tray of plastic coffees.

"I thought we could all use some -," Barker said, his voice trailing off and his eyes meeting Julia's. "You're awake!"

"Barely," Dot said. "She's delirious. Thinks that

dreadful Lewis boy jumped in front of his mad father's blade to save her."

"He did," Julia said, fighting off more coughing. "He is just a boy."

Dot, Sue and Jessie all backed away, making room for Barker to stand by Julia's side. He didn't hesitate in scooping up her hand and when he squeezed, she squeezed back.

"I was so worried about you," Barker said, his bottom lip trembling. "Why did you have to go snooping, hmm?"

"I didn't," Julia said, attempting to laugh but coughing instead. "Not this time. I went to get a prospectus for Jessie. For college."

Jessie looked guiltily to the floor, and Julia tried to tell her she didn't need to feel guilty, but she couldn't summon the energy to raise her voice loud enough to reach her across the room.

"You can explain later," Barker said, his hand clutching Julia's hand so tight she felt safe enough to forget what had happened. "All that matters is you are safe."

"The alarm?" Julia asked.

"It was Vincent's medical alarm," Barker said, with a small laugh. "He saw you and he *saved* you. He pressed the button and woke everyone up. The man is still in there somewhere."

"Katie was telling the truth," Julia croaked, her eyelids fluttering. "The burglar was real – I found – *I found -*,"

Darkness took her once again.

CHAPTER 17

3 WEEKS LATER

J ulia's first day back in the café was a surreal one.
She was given more flowers and sympathy cards
than she knew what to do with, and she
recounted the tale of what had happened so many
times it had started to feel like it had happened to
somebody else. Even though they had all heard the

story on the Peridale grapevine, there wasn't a dry eye or a gasp free mouth in her café that day.

A little after noon, Sally Marriott came into the café alone. All heads turned and watched as she walked towards the counter, her head bowed in silence. When she met Julia's eyes, she immediately broke out into tears.

"Oh, Julia!" she cried. "I feel like all of this is *my* fault."

"Don't be silly," Julia said as she took Sally into the kitchen to get her away from the eavesdroppers. "You didn't have anything to do with this."

"I just can't help but think if I hadn't lied to the police, or to you, maybe the truth would have helped them in some way."

Sally sat down and Julia made her a strong cup of coffee. Sally explained how when she had visited Peridale Manor, she had found Richard pinning Charles to the ground and punching him in the face. She told Julia that she managed to drag him away and convince him to come home with her so they could talk. As they were leaving, they saw Charles fall out of the window, so they quickly left the scene so they wouldn't be suspected.

"I understand," Julia said, resting her hand on Sally's jittery knee. "You don't have to feel guilty."

Sally sipped her coffee and attempted to smile, but Julia could sense sadness still deep within her.

"I really loved him, Julia," she said, nodding her head and holding back tears. "I thought Charles was the one. We met late last year at The Comfy Corner. Richard had stood me up and Charles was supposed to be meeting his sister because she wanted to tell him something, but she didn't show up. I suppose it was about the spa, but she decided against telling him so she could get on with things. If she had just told him, none of this would have happened. He wasn't as bad as people said. We got talking and he was so kind and sensitive in a way Richard wasn't. One thing led to another and – *well*, you know the rest. Richard found messages on my phone the night before the garden party, so he went up to the manor looking for Charles because he knew everybody in the village would be there. I was such a fool, Julia."

"Do you think marrying him is the best decision?"

"I've left him," Sally said, calming herself long enough to take a sip of coffee. "For good, this time. We were never right for each other. I was just in love with the idea of the fairy tale. Cinderella and her Prince Charming. He showed me attention and I fell in love with the fantasy. I'm sorry to cancel my wedding cake order again."

Julia smiled and stood up. She walked over to the fridge and pulled out a plastic box filled with small slices of cake. She peeled off the lid and offered it to Sally, who looked suspiciously at them before plucking one out.

"Cinnamon, rose and orange!" she exclaimed as she bit into it. "Oh, Julia! It's delicious! It's better than I ever could have imagined."

"Keep them," Julia said. "Those three weeks at home gave me plenty of time to practice. I had a feeling you wouldn't be walking down the aisle with Richard, but I wanted to perfect it for my own sake. Now that I have the recipe, you can ask me for that any time. I see where you were coming from. It is an unusual taste, but it's quite refreshing on the palette."

After Sally finished her coffee, she once again exited through the backdoor away from prying eyes. This time, Julia knew Sally was walking towards a better life for herself.

No sooner had Sally left did another unexpected guest arrive. Julia watched as her father walked into her café for the first time. He looked around the room, appearing surprised by what he saw. Jessie scowled at him over her shoulder as she sprayed cleaner on the cake display case.

"You've done a really nice job in here," he said as he walked towards the counter. "What do you recommend?"

"I have your favourite Victoria sponge," Julia said, already reaching into the counter for it.

"I fancy something different today," he said calmly. "It's time for a change."

Julia paused, her hand hovering over the Victoria sponge. She smiled at her father, and he smiled at her. She could feel the first page of their new story being written in that moment. She plucked out a chocolate brownie, added it to a plate with cream, and slid it across the counter.

"On me," Julia said. "How's Katie?"

"Recovering," he said as he ran his finger through the cream and dropped it into his mouth. "Her brother dying, being arrested, and then what happened to those two lads. It's all just hit her hard."

"I need to go to the manor to see her," Julia said, bowing her head. "To apologise for not believing her."

"I didn't either," he said, joining her in bowing his head. "I don't think she's forgiven me for it, but it will take time. I think we've all learned that time can heal old wounds."

"Or reopen them," Jessie chimed in as she scrubbed the front of the counter. "But it can heal them too."

Brian laughed softly and looked down at the brownie, then around the café, and then at Julia. She thought he might cry, but he collected himself and stared deep into her eyes.

"I'm proud of you, kid," he said.

He quickly finished his brownie and left, promising to go and speak to Sue. Julia hoped it wouldn't be the last time he stepped foot in her café.

"Jessie, can you watch the counter for me?" Julia asked as she pulled out a heavy white envelope she had hidden that morning. "I just need to nip next door."

"You got it, boss," Jessie said, saluting with a wink. "I held down this place for three weeks, didn't I? I think the folk around here are starting to warm to my cakes more than yours."

Julia smiled her thanks to Jessie, not wanting to tell her about the dozens of phone calls she had had since Jessie had been in charge, begging her to come back so they didn't have to endure Jessie's baking. It would take a little more practice before she was up to Julia's standards, but now that she was enrolled in her college apprenticeship, she was optimistic for the future.

With the letter clutched in her hands, Julia walked next door to the post office. She thought about how much this letter had been taunting her everyday while she had been at home, mocking her for not having had the guts to get rid of it sooner.

She wondered if that was how Jessie had felt, stuffing all of the letters from the social workers, who were trying to arrange a home visit, in various boots in her wardrobe, all of which Julia had discovered and read. It turned out Jessie's sleepwalking had been from her fear that if faced with the official decision of fostering her, that Julia would reject her. The second Julia told her that wasn't going to happen, they hugged it out and agreed that there would be no more letter hiding or secrets. Jessie agreed on the condition that Julia posted her divorce papers, but that was a condition Julia was more than happy to oblige. The sleepwalking had stopped, and the only thing waking Julia in the night was the banging of her own head when the painkillers wore off.

"First class," Julia said, dropping the heavy envelope onto the scales. "Recorded. I want to make sure this gets where it's going."

"That'll be three pounds twenty please, love,"

said Shilpa, the kind lady who ran the post office. "How's your head?"

Julia's fingers wandered up to the butterfly stitches keeping her healing cut together. She had figured out a way to style her hair so the work of Terry Lewis couldn't be seen even when the stitches were taken off later that afternoon.

"Healing," Julia said as she handed over the exact money in coins. "Can barely feel a thing."

"You've been through the wars, young lady," Shilpa said as she counted out the money. "Your tracking number is on your receipt. Take care, love."

And just like that, her divorce papers were gone. Out of her hands. She had expected to feel euphoric, like a weight had lifted off her shoulders, but instead she felt nothing. It made her wonder why she had dreaded this moment for so long. Jerrad was in her past now, and she had so much to look forward to in her future.

Against the advice of the doctors, Julia drove up to the hospital after the café closed. She was itching to have her stitches taken off, and she didn't fancy chancing her luck trying to make her appointment in time catching the buses.

"One, two, *three*," the nurse said as she peeled

the stitches off. "Didn't hurt, did it?"

"I've been through worse."

The nurse smiled but she didn't question Julia. Unless she had read the lengthy articles about what had happened in *The Peridale Post*, she doubted the nurse would know. Julia was glad. She knew eventually the residents of Peridale would move onto something else, but until that time happened, people weren't letting her forget the ordeal she had been through.

After giving her some aftercare instructions and a prescription for a cream to help the scar fade quicker, Julia left the room but she didn't head for the hospital exit. Instead, she walked into the depths of the hospital to the room where Jamie Lewis was being kept.

Luckily for her, the officer on the door was one of the officers who had originally arrested Katie, so he knew exactly what had happened. He told Julia she could have five minutes, and that was all. She didn't need any more.

She slipped into the room and the noisy hospital corridor faded away. The small body in the bed rolled over, its eyes widening with recognition. He attempted to sit up, but handcuffs chaining him to the bed restricted his movement.

Lemonade and Lies

"How are you feeling?" Julia asked, unsure of what to say, and unable to look him in the eyes.

"Sore," he mumbled. "You?"

"Better."

Julia pulled up a chair and sat next to Jamie. She hadn't brought a card, or flowers, or grapes, but she was there, and she knew that was important. The boy would be going to prison for a long time, so she wanted to make sure he knew exactly how she felt.

"I understand why you did what you did to Charles Wellington," Julia said, looking in his eyes for the first time since he had thrown himself out of the window clutching his father, an image that had haunted her every night since. "I know what it feels like when everybody wants you to be one thing, but you want to be another."

"I never wanted to be a builder," Jamie said, looking hopelessly into Julia's eyes. "I wanted to be a comic book illustrator. I got into a really good college in London, but my dad told me I couldn't go. He said I had to be in his trade because they couldn't afford to send me to London, and they needed the extra hands."

"That wasn't fair of him," Julia said.

"I gave up my dreams to help him and he didn't care. When I heard Charles Wellington talking over the microphone about how he was going to stop the spa being built, I saw everything I had already lost. I ran into the house looking for him. Some guy was hitting him, but a woman came and dragged him away. Charles stumbled upstairs so I followed him. I didn't know what I was going to do. I thought I was going to talk to him, to convince him how other people in the village needed the spa, how *my family* needed the spa. Without that job, we were losing our house. I guess we've lost it now. The debt collectors were days away as it was. We were counting on that money to save us. My dad gambled away everything. Their lifesavings, the money my gran had left for my future. *Everything*. I hated him for it.

"Charles came out of the bathroom, and I tried to talk to him. He called me a dumb kid and he wouldn't listen to what I had to say. I panicked. I saw my father in him. I *cracked*. I picked up the bust and I hit his head. He fell so quickly. I didn't mean to kill him. I didn't mean -,"

"I know," Julia said, reaching instinctively out for Jamie's hand.

He held back the tears before continuing.

"I knew he was dead. I just knew it. My dad came looking for me and he saw what I had done. It was his idea to throw Charles out of the window. He picked him up, and tossed him like he was nothing. We cleaned up the blood and he took the bust. I ran into the bathroom and I panicked. I knew any minute somebody would rush upstairs to see what had happened, so I opened the window and I climbed down the drainpipe.

"And then I ran. I didn't stop running. I never thought I would stop running. My dad came home and he found me. He beat me. Then my mum came home. We didn't tell her. My dad told her that we had gone for some lunch together and it was best she just tell people we were all together when Charles was pushed out of the window. She didn't question him. She didn't find out the truth until my dad hit you. I wanted to keep her out of it, but it was too late.

"When I saw my dad about to stab you, I knew I had caused this. I couldn't let it happen again. I didn't think, I just jumped in front of him. I *wanted* to die. I *wanted* him to die. I *wanted* it all to stop. I thought it had worked. I remember looking up at the rain, and touching the knife handle, and then my eyes closed. When I woke up here, I didn't understand why I wasn't dead."

"There has been *enough* death," Julia said, squeezing his hand. "You took two lives, but you saved one. You already know you're going to prison, but you'll be a free man one day. You might even be out by the time you're my age."

"That old?" Jamie said, laughing through his tears.

"Less of the old," Julia whispered with a wink. "Take care of yourself, Jamie."

"You too."

"If you still remember me when you get out of prison, come and find me," Julia said as she opened the door. "I'll show you what old really means."

She doubted she would ever see Jamie again, but she hoped he would still be able to have a life one day, maybe even find happiness. He was just a child who was pushed to make a bad decision. Julia knew how easily that could have been Jessie on any different day. She looked back at him one last time, almost upset that she had discovered the truth.

"Julia?" she heard Detective Inspector Brown's voice call out down the hallway as she walked away from his room. "What are you doing here?"

Julia turned, a smile on her face and peace in her heart. Seeing Barker warmed her like the hottest July sun.

"Getting closure," she said.

"Did you get it?"

"I think so."

"I'm glad," Barker said, glancing over his shoulder to his colleague who was standing guard outside of Jamie's room. "I slipped him twenty quid and told him to let you in when you finally showed up."

"What made you think I would show up?"

"Because you're a good woman," Barker said, his smile easy and soft. "A good woman, who I still haven't taken on a proper first date."

"I hear the jacket potatoes in the canteen aren't half bad," Julia said, linking arms with Barker and setting off down the corridor.

"I thought you would be sick of hospital food by now," Barker whispered, leaning in and resting his head on hers.

"I am," Julia agreed. "But the company will make up for it."

They walked down the corridor arm in arm, and Julia thought about her happy ending. She knew nothing that ended was happy, but she was on the brink of something new, with Barker and Jessie, and that made her heart truly happy.

If you enjoyed *Lemonade and Lies*, why not sign up to Agatha Frost's **free** newsletter at **AgathaFrost.com** to hear about brand new

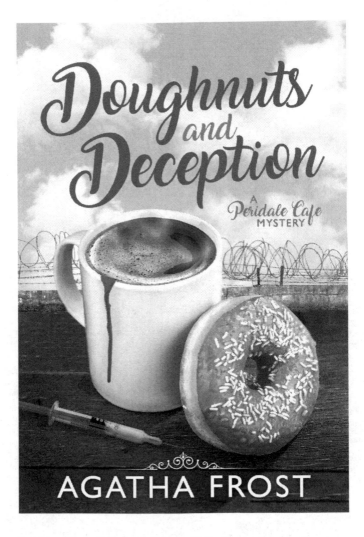

Coming March 2017! Julia and friends are
back for another Peridale Café Mystery case in
Doughnuts and Deception!

Made in the USA
Lexington, KY
12 September 2018